WILD VENOM

TYSON WILD BOOK THIRTY ONE

TRIPP ELLIS

TRIPP ELLIS

1

"What's a girl gotta do to get a drink around here?" she said, the gun still dangling from her hand, the suppressor attached to the threaded barrel.

The tangy scent of gunpowder lingered, and a slight haze filled the passageway.

I gave her a sharp look. "Are you sure you've got time for that? No doubt the neighbors heard the gunshots and called the police. They'll be here shortly."

"I won't stay long. And you're not going to let them arrest me, are you?" she said with a sassy smirk.

Sophia stood in the salon near the entryway to the port-side passage, a dead man oozing blood at her feet. She spun around, sauntered to the bar, and set her pistol on the counter. She moved around the bar, grabbed a glass and a bottle of premium whiskey, and poured herself a drink.

I walked down the hallway, stepped over the body, and entered the salon. Pale shafts of moonlight cut through the darkness, seeping in through the large windows, casting deep shadows.

"You want one?" she asked casually as if there was nothing unusual about having a drink with two dead bodies nearby.

Her demeanor didn't surprise me. I had gotten to know Sophia Breslin pretty well. She was a cold-blooded killer. Emotionless. No feeling. No remorse.

She had changed her look. The stunning vixen was now a platinum blonde—her hair sculpted into a severe, stylish bob. She wore a black fitted long-sleeve shirt, yoga pants, and black sneakers—reasonable attire when prancing around a superyacht in the middle of the night with intent to kill. The tight fabric hugged her petite form, leaving nothing to the imagination. The pants looked painted on, and every delightful curve magnified. Though, she blended in with the darkness.

Sophia was like a shadow herself.

She put the glass to her plump lips and let the smooth amber liquid slide down her throat, leaving a lipstick stain on the glass. She wasn't worried about DNA or fingerprints at this juncture. Her identity was no longer a secret.

She looked at me with a cocky grin, knowing I was interested in what she had to say.

I declined her offer for a drink. With two dead bodies aboard the *Avventura,* one of which was peppered with bullets from my gun, I thought it best not to talk to the sheriff with whiskey on my breath.

"Suit yourself," she said, taking another swig.

"Where is he?" I asked.

"Where is who?"

"No games. You said you knew where Elias Fink was."

She smiled. "I do."

I waited for her to speak, but she didn't. "Are you going to tell me?"

"Maybe. If you play your cards right."

The muscles in my jaw flexed, and a frustrated breath escaped my nostrils.

"Don't get huffy with me. I just saved your ass. You'd have been dead, and Elias's goons would have completed their mission."

I couldn't argue. She saved my ass. There were no two ways about it. "What were you doing creeping around my boat in the middle of the night?"

"Looking out for you."

I scoffed. "Ha. You're my guardian angel now after you once tried to kill me?"

"That was then, this is now," she said with a casual shrug of the shoulder.

"Why the change of heart?"

"I told you. We're on the same team now. Elias sent a hit squad after me. We have a mutual interest in seeing his demise. Am I right?"

Again, I couldn't argue.

"He's a petty, vindictive man," she continued.

"And a dangerous one."

"All the more reason we need to team up and take him down."

"You've lost your mind if you think I'm going to team up with you."

She rolled her eyes and frowned. "Grow up. Move on. What's in the past is in the past. Leave it there. It's water under the bridge."

I lifted an incredulous eyebrow. "Easy for you to say. You tried to kill me. You murdered Cobra Company operatives. You expect me to forget that?"

"It was just business."

"You have a target on your head. People aren't going to forget what you did."

"I know Isabella is mad at me. But I figure if we take out Elias Fink, that wipes the slate clean."

I scoffed again. "I'm not sure the slate can ever be wiped clean."

She looked at me with a pouty face and pleading eyes. She spoke in a baby-doll voice. "What's the matter, Tyson? Don't you believe in second chances? In redemption?"

2

———

I gave her a long look.

"I suppose you think I'm unredeemable. But you and I are not that different. You've killed your fair share. You've done questionable things. You've followed orders when you knew they might not be the right thing to do. We've all done things we regret."

"Everything I've done was in service to my country."

She rolled her eyes. "Justify it however you want. You're still a killer."

"I've changed."

"And so have I," she said in an insincere tone.

"I find that hard to believe."

"We all have our moments of self-reflection." With a sultry gaze, she leaned against the bar counter. "Tell me, what was your moment? Was it almost dying in Mexico?"

My eyes narrowed at her.

"I know more about you than you think."

"A killer should know the target inside and out."

"You are not my target anymore."

We were silent for a moment. The boat rocked gently, and mooring lines creaked.

Sophia continued, "I heard you were technically dead, and they brought you back. Did you see the other side?"

I said nothing.

"I guess that would change a person. But it's not like you eased up on the body count since then, so don't give me any grief."

"I only—"

She cut me off, "Kill people who deserve it?"

"Something like that."

I still gripped my pistol in my hand. I wasn't beyond killing her if she posed a credible threat.

Sophia grabbed her pistol from the bar counter, and my grip tightened.

She unscrewed the suppressor, holstered the subcompact weapon around her angle, then slipped the suppressor into a pouch on a fanny pack.

"You should be nice to me," Sophia said. "I know where the most wanted terrorist in the world is right now. A guy your government has been trying to find for the last 10 years."

"And how did you find him?"

She shrugged again. "I have my ways. You're not the only one with contacts."

"Where is he?"

"He's in Caracas. There's an extradition treaty with Venezuela, but good luck getting any cooperation. I hear Elias is tight with Maduro."

"I want proof."

"How about we go down and kill him, and that will be all the proof you need?"

I shook my head. "I want actionable intel from qualified sources."

"Contact your people. Have them verify it."

The sound of distant sirens warbled, drawing closer.

"I guess that's my cue," Sophia said. "If I get you actionable intel, are you in?"

"Why don't you just take care of Elias yourself?"

"It's always good to have backup. A buddy."

"I'm not your buddy."

"Once we kill Elias Fink, you will be. You'll love me for bringing him to you. You won't have to worry about his hit squads anymore, and neither will I. We'll have done the nation a service. We'll have taken down the most wanted terrorist since bin Laden. They'll write books about us. Make movies. We'll be famous."

"I don't want to be famous."

She laughed. "You, sort of, already are."

Sophia moved from behind the bar and headed toward the sliding glass door of the salon. "I'll get you your proof. Then we'll go down and do the job. Deal?"

"I want my tender back," I said, redirecting. She'd stolen it the last time she was on the *Avventura* and used it as a getaway vehicle.

"I'll give it back. But not today." She slid open the door and hustled across the aft deck to the passerelle, the sound of sirens growing closer. "I'll be in touch," she yelled over her shoulder as she scampered to the dock and trotted to a nearby slip where she'd tied up my tender.

She cast off the lines, hopped on board, and cranked up the engine. Sophia cruised out of the marina just as patrol units pulled into the parking lot. Red and blue lights flickered across the boats.

I watched from the aft deck as the deputies sprang from their vehicles and hustled down the dock toward the *Avventura*.

3

"Who the hell are these ass-clowns, and why are they dead on your boat?" Sheriff Daniels asked.

His annoyed eyes glared at me. The sheriff wasn't a fan of getting pulled out of bed in the wee hours of the morning.

A camera flashed, spilling out of the port-side passageway as a forensic photographer documented the scene. Brenda hovered over the body, wearing pink nitrile gloves. Deputies milled about.

I gave Daniels the story. Most of it, anyway. "I don't have IDs on the thugs. I'm working on that, but it's safe to say this was a hit squad sent by you know who."

I'd sent images of the goons to Isabella for identification. She was my handler at Cobra Company—the premiere clandestine agency that did contract work for the CIA.

The sheriff's eyes narrowed at me. "And you let a known fugitive walk out of here?"

I shrugged sheepishly. "She had a gun. What was I going to do?"

Daniels rolled his eyes. "Tell me again why is it that she saved your ass?"

I shrugged, then deadpanned, "She's clearly infatuated with me."

That earned another eye roll. "She's crazier than you are, Wild."

The dead thugs were loaded into body bags, zipped up, and rolled out on a gurney. When the swarm of investigators cleared out, I swabbed the deck, mopping up the blood-stains. It was something I had to do aboard the boat all too often.

I was up, and there was no going back to sleep. I put on a pot of coffee and fixed breakfast. I took my plate up to the sky-deck and ate as the sun crested the horizon. There was a nice morning breeze, and the amber rays sparkled the teal water. I sat there and tried to enjoy the morning, letting the adrenaline of the attack fade.

Teagan stopped by before her shift and dropped off Buddy and Fluffy. She'd been feeling a little uneasy at her apartment alone and wanted to keep the furballs for a night.

With mesmerizing teal eyes, brown hair, and a petite little figure, Teagan drew more than her fair share of attention. Some of it unwanted. After starring in the music video for Wild Fury's *All I Need*, the occasional fan would turn up unannounced at her apartment, having tracked her down. They were mostly harmless, but it unsettled her. It only takes one psycho.

"They're fed and watered," she said. "I'm happy to take them anytime."

I smiled, knelt down, and petted Buddy. The little Jack Russell was eager to see me. He wagged his tail and licked my face. Fluffy rushed inside, completely ignoring me. She leaped onto the settee and took her usual position as *Queen of the Avventura*. The aloof white cat surveyed her domain for a moment, then began to groom herself.

My phone buzzed with a call. I pulled the device from my pocket as Teagan backed away from the salon door.

"Talk to you later," she said as she spun around and sauntered down the passerelle to the dock. She hustled to *Diver Down*.

She had a nice hustle.

I didn't recognize the call, and I wasn't too fond of answering unknown numbers. I swiped the screen, anyway. "This is Tyson Wild."

"Mr. Wild, my name is Nolan Orton. Tony Scarpetti gave me your number, said you might be able to help me."

Tony Scarpetti was an old Mafia guy who ran a high-stakes poker game at the *Seven Seas*. Despite his dubious past, Tony was a good guy. I'd done a few favors for him, and he'd done a few favors for me. As far as I knew, he was clean now. He had a couple of restaurants on the island, and in my book, there was no better pizza on the planet.

I recognized Nolan's name right away. "*The* Nolan Orton?"

He chuckled. "Yes, *that* Nolan Orton."

My brow crinkled with curiosity. "What can I do for you?"

"Tony informed me that you were the best when it came to handling certain matters. And that you could do so discreetly."

"It depends on what we're talking about."

"I have a dire situation, and I need your expertise. Money is no object, so you can name your price. A positive outcome is my only concern."

My curiosity was piqued. "Cut to the chase. What do you need?"

"I think it's better we discuss this in person. I'll send you my address. Can you be here within a half hour? It's of the utmost importance."

"I'll be there."

"Thank you. I look forward to meeting you."

4

J D swung by the marina in his Miami Blue Porsche and picked me up.

I jogged down the dock and hopped into the passenger seat. The top was down, and the music blasted. I buckled my safety belt and sat back in the chalk leather seats as we cruised across the island to the posh neighborhood of *Stingray Bay*. Wind swirled around the cabin, blowing JD's long blond hair. The turbo engine growled.

Jack wore mirrored aviator shades and his typical uniform, which consisted of a Hawaiian shirt, cargo shorts, and checkered Vans.

"What do you think he wants?"

I shrugged. "Sounded urgent."

"That guy is loaded. I mean, *loaded*, loaded." He paused. "He doesn't want us to do something illegal, does he?"

"He didn't say. But I'm sure he's aware we're deputies, and I have a feeling he's a pretty smart guy. You don't get to be in his position if you're a dumbass."

"Never underestimate luck. Being in the right place at the right time beats bad timing and intelligence."

We twisted through the streets of the upscale neighborhood, cruising past perfectly manicured yards and trimmed hedgerows. Luxury cars and SUVs were parked in circular driveways. Crews of lawn care professionals blew leaves, edged driveways and sidewalks, and tended to the landscaping. Palm trees swayed overhead, and canals snaked their way behind the homes. They were filled with luxury yachts, sailboats, speedboats, and other expensive watercraft.

We pulled to the curb in front of Nolan Orton's house at 1214 Anglers Way. It was a stunning home. There was no doubt about it. But the multimillion-dollar estate seemed somewhat pedestrian for a man of Nolan Orton's wealth. He was on the list of the richest men in America. As the CEO of the social media giant *Flutter*, he'd amassed an unbelievable amount of wealth within a few short years. The company was experiencing exponential year-over-year growth and was on pace to knock off platforms like Twitter and Facebook.

His property was surrounded by a privacy wall that was 8 feet high. None of the other homes in the neighborhood had one, and the wall was constructed at Orton's request. I had no doubt that a large contribution to the homeowners association got the board to look the other way and ignore the deed restrictions.

There were two silver SUVs parked at the curb in front of the home. The driveway was gated, and so was the main walkway.

JD pulled to the curb across the street, and we hopped out of the Porsche and ambled to the gate. I rang the video doorbell, and Orton's voice crackled through the speaker a moment later. "Deputy Wild?"

That answered my question about whether or not he knew we were officers of the law. I flashed my shiny gold shield to the camera. "This is my partner Deputy Jack Donovan."

JD smiled and waved.

Nolan buzzed us into the courtyard, and we ambled up the walkway to the front porch. I noted multiple security cameras around the premises.

A stocky gentleman in a grey suit pulled open the front door. He was mid 30s with a slick bald head and a square jaw. He had a dimple in his chin and was the kind of guy that had a 5 o'clock shadow a minute after he shaved. His nose looked like it had taken a few punches, and his blue eyes were narrow and calculating. He had an Eastern European look to him. He looked like he'd seen action—definitely former military. He didn't look like the kind of guy that took crap from anybody.

He extended his hand and shook with a firm grasp. "I'm Jason Bradley, head of security."

We made introductions.

"Come on in," he said. "Nolan is waiting."

He motioned us inside and closed the door behind us after scoping out the courtyard, his watchful eyes always on the lookout.

He led us across the marble tile into the living room with high vaulted ceilings and large windows that allowed copious amounts of light to bathe the interior. The home was elegantly decorated with modern white leather furniture. The dark grey hardwoods in the living room contrasted well with the French gray walls and white trim. Large canvases of fine art adorned the living room. There was a beautiful pool in the backyard. The clear water glimmered with sunlight, and spires of tall narrow evergreens lined the edge of the pool like columns. Beyond the pool was a canal and what I assumed was Nolan's 132-foot *SunTrekker* yacht. Again, a nice boat, but not as decadent as I would have imagined for a man of Nolan's wealth.

Orton stood up from the couch and greeted us with a solemn face. He had short dark hair, light brown eyes, and a narrow face. He wore stylish glasses with thick black frames, a black fitted shirt, and gray slacks. He was thin and fit and stood about 6 feet tall. His skin looked like he just had a facial. It was smooth and vibrant. His eyebrows were manicured, and his hair quaffed to perfection.

"Thanks for coming. I'm sorry I couldn't be more specific on the phone, but I didn't want to take any chances."

"What seems to be the problem?" I asked. "And how can we help?"

"It's my wife... She's missing."

5

"How long has she been gone?" I asked.

"Yesterday afternoon," Nolan said.

"What time?"

"I don't know exactly. I'm guessing between 3 and 4 PM."

"Has she ever run off like this before?"

Nolan hesitated and exchanged a tense glance with Jason. His worried eyes reconnected with mine. "I'm not sure she ran off. I'm concerned she was kidnapped."

"Have you received a ransom demand?"

"No."

"Any communication from the possible kidnappers?"

"No."

"What makes you think she was taken?"

"Gut instinct. This is totally out of character for Eva. She wouldn't leave without telling someone. She never goes anywhere without a security detail. I forbid it."

I lifted a curious brow.

"You have to understand, I receive countless death threats on a daily basis from disgruntled users. As one of the fastest-growing social networks, we have an extraordinarily high customer satisfaction and engagement ranking, but we can't please everyone. As you are no doubt aware, I am a high-net-worth individual. That makes my family a prime target for kidnapping and extortion. We try to take every precaution, but yesterday there was a SNAFU."

"I noticed security cameras on the way in," I said. "And I see several throughout the house."

"The perimeter is secured with cameras," Jason said. "But we ran into a bit of a glitch with the system. There was a power surge during the recent storm, and even with surge suppression, it knocked out the home network. There was a direct lightning strike."

"The whole system has been down for a few days," Nolan said. "There is no security footage."

"Tell me about your security team."

"I have a security staff of 16. *Had*," Nolan corrected. "We're at 15 now."

"Had?"

"I let an employee go."

I lifted another curious brow.

Nolan continued. "My former Head of Security, Liam Nash."

A staffing change sparked alarm bells right away.

"We work in four-man teams," Jason said, "doing six-hour shifts."

"I find six hours allows for peak performance," Nolan said. "More than that, attention starts to wane."

"So, normally, you have four guards at the house, 24 hours a day."

"Yes."

"Surely one of your staff can speak to Eva's whereabouts at the time of her disappearance?"

"That's the SNAFU," Nolan said. "Since I had fired Liam, that left us short-staffed. I had a meeting to attend yesterday. I left the house with Will and Toby. Jason stayed behind with Eva." His eyes filled. "I should never have left her alone."

"It's my fault," Jason said. "I take full responsibility."

My eyes fell upon Jason.

"Eva begged me to run an errand for her," Jason explained. "I told her I couldn't leave her at home by herself. But she didn't want to ride with me."

"So you left Eva alone in the house between 3 and 4 PM yesterday, correct?"

Jason nodded. "She wanted me to pick up a dress from *Biagi Couture* and a gallon of chocolate chip mint ice cream on my way home. I mistakenly thought the next detail would arrive shortly."

"It's not your fault Jason," Nolan said. "I'm well aware of how difficult it is to say no to my wife. She can be very demanding at times," he said, choosing his words carefully.

There was a picture of Nolan with a beautiful blonde on the coffee table. I picked up the silver frame and studied the photo. "I assume this is Eva?"

He nodded.

The girl was nothing short of perfection—blue eyes, pouty lips, perfect skin, symmetrical features. Eva graced the pages of catalogs as a former lingerie model. She had style and sophistication, and her sultry gaze could heat things up quicker than a nuclear detonation. I could understand Nolan's distress. Eva was the kind of woman you'd do anything to get back if she went missing.

"When did you fire Liam?" I asked.

"Last week."

"Why?"

6

Nolan hesitated and exchanged another glance with Jason before answering. "I suspected they were having an affair."

The words dribbled from his mouth, and he hung his head and sighed. He seemed both crushed and embarrassed.

"So, let me get this straight," I said. "Your former Head of Security is engaged in extracurricular activities with your wife, and you fired him. Within a week, your wife goes missing. I'm thinking Liam Nash could be a person of interest. Is it possible she ran away with him?"

Nolan was silent for a long moment. The thought was a bitter pill to swallow, I'm sure. "I've considered that."

"Have you reached out to him?"

"No."

"I'm sure you've tried calling your wife?"

"Her phone is here. She wouldn't leave without it."

"How long has your wife been having an affair with Liam?"

Nolan stammered. "I don't know. I think I had blinders on for a long time. I felt like something wasn't right, but I ignored it. I noticed subtle glances between the two. The way they'd laugh together. Little touches between them. I dismissed it. And the few times I brought it up, Eva turned the tables and made it seem like I was some kind of paranoid psychopath. She even accused me of cheating."

"Were you?"

Nolan's face crinkled. "Who in their right mind would step out on a woman like Eva?"

"If things were heating up between Eva and Liam, I assume they were cooling off between you two in the bedroom?"

"I don't see how that's any of your business," Nolan said, taking offense.

"I'm just trying to get a full picture of the situation."

Nolan's entire body was tense. He forced himself to relax and exhaled a breath. "I'm sorry. I understand you need as much information as possible. You'll have to forgive me. My nerves are beyond frazzled."

"Do you know if Eva is in love with Liam?"

It was a painful question. He sucked in a breath, held it, then exhaled again. "I don't know. That's a distinct possibility." He slumped like a sad puppy dog. "I just want her back. I don't care what she's done. I just want a chance to fix our marriage and put our life back together."

"We'll talk to Liam and see if he knows anything. I'll need a list of your entire security team as well as household staff and anyone else who may have access to the premises—lawn care professionals, maintenance crews, cleaning staff."

Nolan nodded. "Jason can provide you with all of that information."

"We'll report her as missing and put out a BOLO," I said.

"I don't want this getting out to the press yet. If she has run off with Liam, I don't want this splashed all over the tabloids."

"I understand." I didn't mention we had a leak within the department. Paris Delaney and her news crew seemed to know about events almost before they happened.

"Tony told me what you did for him," Nolan said. "He said if you can't find Eva, nobody can."

"Try to stay calm. For all we know, she just needed a little personal time. She could have planned her escape, sent Jason on an errand, and is sitting in a posh hotel right now getting a spa treatment."

"I'd like to believe that. But Eva would never leave her phone. The damn thing was an extension of herself."

"If she's having an affair, you need to consider the possibility that she has a burner phone."

He cringed. "Right."

"We'll do everything we can."

He forced a grim nod. "I trust that you will."

"Where's the rest of your security staff?"

"I thought it best we had this discussion in private." Nolan looked at his watch. "The rest of my security detail should arrive shortly if you'd like to speak with them."

"I want to talk to everyone. What about executive assistants, personal chefs, etc.?"

"I value my privacy, so I don't keep a full-time kitchen staff—only for special occasions. Harlow is my personal assistant. She helps with scheduling, keeping the home fully stocked and functional, and keeps me on time to appointments."

"Where is she now?"

"She should be here soon."

"Was she present the day of Eva's disappearance?"

"She was with me at the time. She's usually glued to my hip during business hours."

"Tell me a little more about your basic security setup."

"I'll let Jason give you a rundown."

"We usually have two security personnel outside, walking the perimeter, and two inside. We keep the spaces in front of the house occupied at all times so no one parks a car bomb at the curb. The walls and windows of the home are bullet-proof. All of the cars have reinforced doors and bulletproof windows. The vehicles are equipped with run-flat tires. There is a panic room in both the bedroom and Mr. Orton's home office. We routinely practice emergency evacuation drills. Unfortunately, there was a gap in our security yesterday, and I take full responsibility."

"Stop beating yourself up over it," Nolan said. "We need to move forward and focus on finding Eva. I should have made sure there was a replacement for Liam. If I would have done so, there wouldn't have been a gap. I'm as much to blame as anyone."

I was surprised that he was willing to take some of the blame. In my experience, people in his position were always looking for a scapegoat.

"Tell me how the gap occurred."

"I thought the next security detail would arrive at the house momentarily," Jason said. "Unfortunately, I had forgotten about the schedule change. They came on duty an hour later than normal."

"Why was there a schedule change?" I asked.

"Keenan, one of the security staff, had a dentist appointment that morning, and we pushed the schedule an hour," Jason said. "I simply forgot."

"An unfortunate confluence of events led to this situation," Nolan quickly added. "Dwelling on the past isn't going to change anything. So where do we go from here?"

7

"Just sit tight," I said. "We'll handle this."

Nolan's face tensed. "I don't like feeling helpless."

"Nobody does." I paused. "I know it's an uncomfortable question, but was the staff aware of your wife's affair?"

Nolan looked at Jason.

The bodyguard shrugged sheepishly. "I think we all suspected it."

"And nobody said anything to Mr. Orton?"

"It was a difficult position to be in," Jason said. "I find it best to stay out of the personal lives of my clients."

He had a point.

I called the sheriff and updated him on the situation.

Jason gave me a list of the security guards and staff. It wasn't long before two of them arrived—Will Davies and Toby

Pearson. I pulled them aside and interviewed the two body-guards in the parlor about yesterday's events.

Will was skinny and tall with short brown hair and a narrow face. Toby was a big bruiser. His navy blue suit looked like it was going to burst at the seams. He wore his sandy-blond hair in a tight crew cut.

Their stories mirrored what Nolan and Jason had said.

"Do you two always escort Nolan when he ventures out of the house?" I asked.

"No," Toby said. "We rotate. Really, it's whoever's available. Nolan likes to avoid routines as much as possible. We change routes, drivers, vehicles. We try to keep a good variation."

"Were you aware of the affair?" I asked.

They both tensed and exchanged a glance, then answered in unison. "We suspected."

"How well do you know Liam?" I asked.

"We'd been working with him for over a year," Toby said. "He was on top of things and easy to get along with. I thought he was crazy when he started diddling the missus."

"This is a great gig," Will said. "Pay is awesome. We get benefits, and Nolan is a good guy."

"Seemed stupid to screw that up," Toby said. "But maybe Liam thought he'd run away with Eva and get half of Nolan's money."

"Have you spoken with him since he was let go?" I asked.

"That's verboten," Will said. "There is a strict no-contact policy regarding that guy. Nolan said anyone who talks to, or hangs out with, Liam is fired on the spot."

"Can't say I blame him for feeling that way," Toby said. "I wouldn't want my security staff associating with the guy who was banging my wife." Toby glanced around to make sure no one was in earshot. He straightened up and cleared his throat. "You'll have to forgive me. I shouldn't have phrased it that way."

"Were you aware that the schedule had been changed yesterday?"

"We all were, but I didn't give it any thought. Nolan had a meeting, and we escorted him to it."

"When we left, Jason said he had a handle on things," Will added.

I asked them a few more questions, then wrapped up. I told Nolan we would be in contact and to let me know if he heard anything from Eva.

We ambled down the walkway, pressed the button, and buzzed open the gate. We stepped outside the compound and climbed into the Porsche. JD cranked up the engine, and we shared a look.

"It would drive me nuts to have all those people around all the time," JD said. "He's like a prisoner of his own success."

"At least he has a nice cage."

JD put the car into gear and pulled away from the curb.

We headed across the island to *Neptune's Cove,* hoping to catch up with Liam Nash.

The former Head of Security lived on a 30-foot sailboat. The marina was on the west side of the island and was home to an array of motor yachts, sport-fishing boats, and sailboats. It was a nice place but a far cry from the luxury of *Stingray Bay.*

JD pulled into the lot and found a spot. He killed the engine, and we walked to the dock, the sun beaming down. Gulls hung on the draft, squawking as we searched the slips for Liam's boat, the *Guardian Angel.*

8

W e found Liam working on his boat. I flashed my badge and made introductions.

"What can I do for you, gentlemen?"

Liam wore white deck shorts and a pale blue short-sleeve collared shirt. He was a handsome man with dark wavy hair, ice-blue eyes, and a square jaw. He had a couple days worth of stubble and could have easily been a model. He had an athletic frame and certainly did his share of bicep curls.

"When was the last time you spoke with Eva Orton?"

He gave me a sour look. "That's not illegal, is it?"

"Not last time I checked," I said.

"Did Nolan put you up to harassing me?"

"We're not harassing you. Just asking a few questions."

"I don't have to answer any of your questions."

"No, you don't. But you might want to."

"Why is that?"

"You were about to tell us the last time you spoke with Eva," I said, ignoring his question.

"Yesterday morning. Why?"

"And you haven't seen her since?"

Liam's face tensed. "What's going on? Is there some kind of problem?"

"Eva is missing," I said. "She wouldn't happen to be here with you, would she?"

His face twisted with concern. "No. She's not."

"You mind if we look around your boat and see for ourselves?"

His worried eyes flicked between the two of us. "What do you mean she's missing?"

"Do you need me to define the term for you?"

He glared at me. "No, I don't need you to define the term. How long has she been gone?"

"Yesterday afternoon."

"Eva wouldn't just run off without telling me. When you say missing, you mean taken."

I exchanged a glance with JD.

"We can't confirm that yet," I said.

Panic washed over Liam. His eyes widened, and his face went long. Either he was genuinely concerned, or he was a damn good actor. "Have there been any ransom demands?"

"No. Right now, she's just missing."

Liam's fear quickly gave way to anger. His jaw flexed, and his hands balled into fists. His face reddened, and the veins in his temples pulsed. "Goddamnit! How did it happen?"

I told him about the situation.

"Jason left her alone?!" he said with astonishment. He frowned, and a few more obscenities slipped from his lips. "Nolan can say what he wants about me, but at least I kept Eva safe."

"When was the last time you spoke with Eva?"

"I texted her last night. She never returned the message. That wasn't unusual. She's not always available to reply. But we usually touch base once a day. I had a funny feeling this morning when I hadn't heard from her."

"How long were you having an affair?"

He hesitated. "Cat's out of the bag now. I guess it doesn't matter. Six months. And don't look at me like that. Nolan was fooling around on Eva."

"Two wrongs don't make a right," JD muttered.

Liam shot him a look.

"Are you sure Nolan was having an affair?"

Liam laughed. "Please. I was with the guy all the time. I knew all of his dirty little secrets."

"And I'm sure you were happy to tell Eva all about them."

He glared at me. "I spent a lot of time with Eva. Things just happened. We became close. It's not just a sexual thing between us."

"So, you love her?"

"Yeah, I do. So what? I'm not the first guy to fall in love with somebody else's wife. Let me tell you, that douchebag doesn't deserve a woman like Eva. I don't care how much money he's got."

"Are you sure you didn't help Eva disappear? Are you sure she's not here with you right now?"

He gave us an exasperated look. "Come aboard. See for yourself."

We crossed the gangway and stepped into the cockpit. It was an older boat, but Liam kept it in good shape. He showed us into the cabin, and we climbed below deck. It was a 2004 fiberglass monohull, updated with the latest navigation and charting. There was a full galley, a head with a shower, a forward V-berth, and an aft guest berth.

We took a look around, and it didn't take long to see that Eva wasn't here. There weren't any articles of women's clothing lying around. No bags. Nothing to indicate she was staying here.

"Satisfied?" Liam asked.

"For the time being."

"What are you doing to find her?"

"Talking to people like yourself. Chasing down leads. The county has been alerted."

Liam shook his head. "She's not missing. She's been abducted. You know how many people have a motive to kidnap Eva? Do you know how much money Nolan has? Eva is a prime target. She didn't just up and disappear."

9

I asked Liam, "Do you know if she is seeing anyone else?"

His face twisted. "No! She isn't seeing anybody else."

"How can you be so sure?"

"Because she's not," he snapped, clearly irritated. "We are in love. She's planning on leaving Nolan."

"For you?"

His eyes narrowed at me. "Yes. For me."

"And how do you see that working out? Seems to me she is accustomed to a certain lifestyle." I gave a casual glance around at the surroundings that were slightly less than luxurious.

Liam didn't like my tone one bit. I was trying to get a reaction out of him. It was working.

"For your information, Eva doesn't care about money. And in a divorce, she's gonna walk away with half. I don't think she's got anything to worry about."

"What about you? Do you care about money?"

His eyes narrowed. "We all care about money to a certain degree, don't we? But I've done okay for myself. I spent a lot of time around some of the richest men in the world. I picked up a lot of little tidbits here and there. I heard conversations. I've been privy to meetings with CEOs of start-tups. I paid attention, I learned to play the game, and I invested very well."

"Sounds like insider trading."

"Sounds like what the rich do on a daily basis. They collude with all their little buddies and move markets. I got myself a piece of it."

"You were the Head of Security for how long?"

"A little over a year."

"What can you tell me about the ongoing security threats?"

"My job was to oversee the logistics of the security detail, make plans and preparations in case of crisis situations. The online security team provided us with daily briefings of any online statements made on the platform that were directed toward Nolan or his family. We would vet those threats and assess a credibility level. Most of them were nonsense."

"What do you think about Jason Bradley? Is he up to the task of Head of Security?"

Liam frowned. "Obviously not. I never would have left Eva alone."

"If Eva was kidnapped, any ideas spring to mind?"

Liam's lips tensed, then he blew out a frustrated breath. "I don't know. With Nolan's net worth, it could be anybody—cartels, terrorist groups, somebody with a vendetta."

"Anybody come to mind?"

He thought for a moment. "I know he's getting sued right now."

"By whom?"

"I don't know all the details. You'll have to ask him."

"What about disgruntled employees?"

Liam glared at us. "I get it. I'm a person of interest given the situation. I'm telling you, I don't know where Eva is. And I would never do anything to harm her."

"What about the corporate side?"

He thought for a moment. "There was a big scandal with their CFO, Evan Voigt. He was embezzling funds. They caught him, and he was fired. I think they came to a non-prosecution agreement as long as he agreed to repay all the money he stole."

"Do you know how much?"

"Ask Nolan. It was a lot."

I dug into my pocket and handed him a card. "If you can think of anything that might be helpful, please get in touch."

"That's it? You just expect me to sit around while you guys chase your tail?"

"Until we have confirmation that Eva's been abducted, she'll be treated as a missing person. At this time, Nolan wants to keep it out of the press."

"I don't give a shit what Nolan wants. I want to find Eva. And I'm going to do everything in my power to locate her."

"All I ask is that you contact the Sheriff's Department if you discover any pertinent information. If she has been abducted, I don't want you taking matters into your own hands."

"There's no doubt in my mind she's been abducted," Liam said.

He looked like a capable guy. And I think his concern for Eva was genuine.

"If you truly care about Eva, you will coordinate your efforts with law enforcement," I said.

I felt a little hypocritical making the statement since JD and I often took a maverick approach to situations. We tended to look at certain rules as *flexible.*

Liam sighed and gave a reluctant nod.

We climbed to the cockpit and crossed the gangway to the dock.

Liam called after us. "There is something else. Probably not related, but there was a guy that showed up at Nolan's house a few weeks ago. Somehow he got past the security system and got access to Nolan."

"On your watch?" I asked.

He frowned and gave a reluctant nod.

"What happened?"

Liam shook his head dismissively. "He was just some guy looking for a job or something like that. We secured the situation, called you guys, and he was arrested and charged with trespassing."

"You recall his name?"

Liam bit his lip as he thought. "Callum Anders."

10

My phone buzzed with a call from Nolan. I swiped the screen and put the phone to my ear as we walked down the dock to the parking lot.

"I just got a text on an encrypted messaging app from someone claiming to have Eva." His voice quivered.

I grimaced. "Did they make any demands?"

"No. They just said to await further instructions and not to contact the police. "

"Do you recognize the number?"

"No."

"Send me the number and screenshots of the text."

"Ok. Did you speak with Liam?"

"Eva's not with him. I don't think he's involved. But he did mention a few persons of interest. What can you tell me about Evan Voight?"

He groaned. "Our HR manager handled his termination. You think this could be some form of retaliation?"

"Could be. Maybe he kidnapped your wife in order to fund the restitution."

"I seriously doubt Evan is capable, but you never know."

"What about Callum Anders?"

"That's the gentleman that showed up at the house, looking for a job. I mean, I gotta appreciate his initiative, but it was inappropriate. We had him arrested and charged with trespassing. You think he could be involved?"

"I think anyone you've had negative contact with is a person of interest. Just try to remain calm. When you hear from the kidnappers again, I want you to get proof of life."

"Proof of life?"

"I know it's an unpleasant thought. But we need to establish that they actually have Eva in their possession and that she is alive and unharmed."

"Oh, God. I don't even want to think about it."

"Have you responded to their text message?"

"No, I wanted to speak with you first."

"Good. We'll be there momentarily."

I ended the call. A moment later, Nolan sent a text with a screenshot of the message from the kidnappers and their phone number. I sent the information to Isabella and asked her to track the number and log the incoming calls to Nolan's phone.

We hopped into the Porsche and sped across the island to *Stingray Bay*. I updated Sheriff Daniels along the way. This officially went from a missing person's case to a kidnapping.

Jason buzzed us into the compound when we arrived and greeted us at the door. He escorted us into the living room. Nolan's assistant, Harlow, was at his side. Will and Toby walked the grounds.

Nolan looked relieved to see us. "What do you want me to do?"

I instructed Nolan to respond to the kidnappers and ask for proof of life. He did so, and we waited for a response.

The room was thick with tension. Nolan fidgeted nervously.

Worry tensed Harlow's pretty face. She was a cute girl—25, shoulder-length caramel hair, azure eyes, olive skin. She had a light dusting of freckles across her nose, and she wore a stylish pinstriped navy pantsuit. The fashionable cut teased at what was underneath.

Her job was to manage Nolan's day and anticipate his every need. It bordered on an obsession. She had empathetic eyes and was keenly aware of those around her. Harlow was an attractive woman, no question. I wondered how many of Nolan's *needs* she was willing to satisfy.

A minute went by with no response from the kidnappers.

Then 2...

Then 10...

Then 20...

Nolan paced about the living room, unraveling. "I don't understand. Why aren't they responding? Does this mean they don't actually have her?"

"It means they can't or won't respond," I said. "Don't read too much into it. Perhaps it's a control issue. They'll respond in their own time. They want you to feel scared, uneasy, and anxious."

"Well, if they expect to get any money out of me, they need to prove to me that she's alive and unharmed," he growled, puffing up in a moment of false bravado. In his frustration, he sent another text message to the kidnappers stating just that.

I cringed. I wanted him to maintain the impression of being calm, cool, and collected—not panicked or desperate.

We waited another few moments, but there was still no response.

This was a clear indication to me that these people were going to do things on their timetable. They weren't going to answer questions. They would just bark commands.

I got the feeling we weren't dealing with amateurs.

11

The FBI typically gets involved in kidnapping cases when the victim is transported across state lines or the crime occurs within the special maritime jurisdiction, the special aircraft jurisdiction, or the victim is a child of tender years. There are a few other scenarios in which they will get involved, but they are always willing to provide support to local law enforcement. Rarely do the Feds *take over* a case.

With the high-profile nature of the victim, I suspected they might want to take a more active role. But it was early, and not many outside of this room knew about the situation. We still hadn't confirmed that Eva had actually been abducted. Depending on the outcome, various agencies would either be fighting to take credit or wanting to steer clear of the debacle.

We waited for the kidnappers to reply, but there was no more communication. They'd have to state their demands at some point. Until then, it was a waiting game.

"I understand you're getting sued," I said.

Nolan frowned. "Another frivolous suit from a leach trying to siphon some of my wealth. Weston Prescott. The suit was dismissed."

"What was the claim?"

"He tried to say that Flutter was his idea. It wasn't. I had a brief meeting with him many years ago, but Flutter was already in development at the time. He discussed things that we had already been working on."

"How much was he asking for?"

"Half the value of the company. I'm happy to say he won't be getting a penny of my money."

"Unless he kidnapped Eva," I said.

Nolan's eyes rounded. "You think he's responsible?"

"You know him better than I do."

Nolan pondered the scenario. "He's a tech guy, not a para-military expert trained in high-value asset abduction. But by all means, if you think it's a viable lead, please pursue it."

"We will. Do you have contact information for him?"

"I can get that for you," Harlow said.

She scrolled through her phone and found Weston's contact info. She asked for my number, then texted me Weston's.

The department didn't have the resources for a dedicated crisis management unit. We were it. Even if we did have a crisis unit, I got the impression Nolan didn't want his house swarming with deputies—especially after he was instructed not to alert the authorities.

We dealt with a lot of missing persons in the area, most of which turned up in a few days. But kidnappings for ransom were rare. We'd dealt with a few in the past. But the most common situation was a non-custodial parent taking their child without permission.

JD was getting antsy and wanted to grab something to eat. My belly was rumbling too. I told Nolan to contact me as soon as he heard from the kidnappers. I figured we'd chase down some of these leads after lunch.

Isabella had called and told me she couldn't trace the kidnapper's phone. The message came through the internet and had been routed through dozens of proxy servers across the globe through a VPN (Virtual Private Network). Whoever was behind this knew how to cover their tracks. Criminals were getting more and more sophisticated everyday.

We left the compound and headed across the island to Oyster Avenue. JD parked at the curb, and we strolled the sidewalk, looking for something to suit our fancy.

A bus passed by wrapped with an advertisement for *Ultra Mega 2*. Jack's daughter, Scarlett, was featured prominently in her tight superhero costume. It was the biggest movie in the country.

JD beamed with pride.

The billboards and ads were everywhere, and the trailer was in constant rotation. The early numbers were good, and the studio had really gotten behind the picture. It was projected to top $1 billion at the box office.

"I think she's going places," JD said with a grin.

"I think she is."

Jack decided to spring for lunch at *Five Fathoms*. We'd been meaning to eat there for a while and kept getting side-tracked. It was a five-star restaurant, and the price reflected its status.

A hostess in formal attire seated us. The decor was elegant and modern. Sconces with blue LED lights colored the walls. Tables were covered with white cloths and lined with fancy black chairs. A bar at the center of the restaurant offered a selection of fine liquor, and the wine cellar could run the tab into the five-figure range if you were feeling spendy. Needless to say, we were underdressed for the occasion. But they weren't as picky at lunch. We'd never have been seated in the evening looking like this.

Smooth downtempo music filtered through speakers, forks clinked against plates, and the murmur of conversation filled the air.

"Your server will be with you shortly," the hostess said before darting away. "Enjoy your meal."

We perused the menu, and a server brought glasses of water. We were greeted by a cute waitress a few moments later. She had straight golden-blonde hair pulled back into a ponytail. The girl had tawny eyes, full lips, and classic features. She flashed a bright smile. "How are you gentlemen this afternoon?"

"Fine, thank you," JD said.

"My name is Amber. I'll be your server today. If there's anything you need, please don't hesitate to ask. Are you gentlemen with ETC?"

"No, we're locals," I said.

"Even better. But don't tell anyone, and I'll give you the ETC discount."

JD smiled. "We like discounts."

ETC was the annual Energy Technology Conference. Thousands of energy professionals from across the globe would flock to the island for a week of conferences, cocktail parties, and expensive dinners. Vendors would showcase new technology, software, and hardware. Discussions would take place about the current state of the industry and future trends. Movers and shakers would no doubt collude to manipulate markets.

For the last few years, the *Seven Seas* had been home to the event. Along with the convention came an influx of *companions* for hire. You could find them loitering around the bar or lounging poolside. It was a lucrative event, and the convention attendees had plenty of disposable income. Some of the wives had caught on and made sure to attend the otherwise boring conference every year. But for many, the week in Coconut Key was like a week in Vegas. What happened at the *Seven Seas* stayed at the *Seven Seas*.

"We have some wonderful specials today," Amber continued. "We have a 7-ounce Western Australian lobster tail topped with shrimp scampi, served with grilled asparagus and roasted potatoes. We also have an 8-ounce center cut filet mignon topped with lump crab meat and béarnaise sauce, served with sautéed mushrooms and roasted potatoes."

Jack smiled. "Sounds delish. I'll take the lobster tail."

"I'll take the filet," I said. "Medium rare."

"Excellent choices. You won't be disappointed. Can I start you off with an appetizer? Calamari, charred octopus, jumbo shrimp?"

"Calamari," JD said.

"A cup of lobster bisque for me."

We bypassed our usual serving of whiskey due to the circumstances.

The waitress collected the menus and scampered away.

"What do you make of this whole scenario?" JD asked.

I shrugged.

"Why no ransom demand yet?"

"Maybe they're trying to figure out how much to ask for. The guy is worth 67 billion, with a *B*. I would imagine he could easily put his hands on tens of millions by the end of the day. Do you ask for a reasonable number that he's inclined to pay quickly? Or do you ask for $1 billion or more?"

"That is a difficult question. I mean, if you ask for a million and he pays it right away, you might feel like a chump, thinking you missed out."

"They also want to control the narrative. They'll make Nolan sweat. Soften him up."

"I think he's already pretty softened up," JD said. "Think she's still alive?"

"She is their insurance policy. Without her, they don't get any money. I'm sure he'll get proof of life along with the ransom demand soon. They'll probably give him a crypto wallet address to make the payment to, and that might be the last he hears from them until she's released."

"Do you really think they'll let her go if he pays?"

"I think that comes down to whether or not she can identify them. If she can't, there's no reason to hang on to her once they get the money. But then again, people often get para-noid in these situations. They're looking at a life sentence either way if they get caught. Murder doesn't add much to the charge."

JD frowned.

Our waitress brought out the calamari, and we snacked until our entrées arrived. The bisque was creamy and smooth with lumps of fresh lobster. Just after we devoured the starters, Amber set our entrées down in front of us. The presentation was beautiful, and it smelled divine.

Amber asked me to cut into my steak to make sure it was cooked to my liking. I sliced through the tender meat with a serrated steak knife, revealing a juicy reddish-pink center cooked to perfection.

"Is there anything else I can get for you?"

"No, thank you," Jack said.

"Enjoy your meal."

Amber darted away, and I sliced off a piece and shoveled it into my mouth. Garlic butter and lemon pepper swirled. It was definitely one of the best steaks on the island.

JD seemed to enjoy his lobster.

We chowed down and filled our bellies. Amber brought the check when we were ready, and JD paid the tab. Without liquor and with the ETC discount, we managed to keep the bill under $200—an impressive feat at this place.

Jack stuffed a wad of cash in the leather folio, and we rolled ourselves out of the restaurant.

It was back to reality.

I figured it was time to track down Callum Anders. He didn't really fit the profile, but it was worth rattling his cage. I called Denise at the Sheriff's Department and she gave me his information.

We found the Porsche, climbed in, and headed across the island.

12

"What do you want?" Callum asked when he pulled open the door to his apartment.

His annoyed eyes flicked between the two of us from behind thick, black-framed glasses. He lived on the third floor of the *Shearwater Apartments*. A nice complex, but nothing too fancy. Callum was a short, round guy with a chubby face and bushy brown hair. He was in his late 20s, had a couple days' worth of stubble, and his chin seemed to disappear into his neck. He wore shorts and a T-shirt, and I detected the distinct odor of marijuana wafting from his apartment.

I gazed beyond him down the entrance foyer into the living room. Sounds from the TV spilled down the corridor. From what I could tell, he'd been sitting around all morning playing video games.

"We'd like to talk to you about Eva Orton," I said.

Callum groaned. "Why are you guys still hassling me about that? I wasn't trespassing. It was a business meeting."

"A business meeting that you didn't have an appointment for."

He shook his head dismissively. "Whatever. You gotta be bold if you want to get anywhere in life. I took my shot. It didn't work out. The guy is a dick for pressing charges."

"Sounds like you're pretty pissed off about that."

"No. I'm ecstatic about having criminal charges on my record," he said flatly.

"What do you know about Eva Orton?"

"I know the bitch is hot. I'll tell you that."

"Did you see her the day that you were trespassing?"

"I wasn't trespassing. I was trying to pitch Nolan an idea that could make us both a lot of money."

"He said you were looking for a job."

"I'm not looking for a job. I got a job. I'm looking to make some serious bank."

"What's your idea?"

"I'm not telling you."

I rolled my eyes.

"I'm ahead of the curve on this. All I need to do is execute. It's a guaranteed success. I just need the startup capital."

"How much capital?"

His eyes narrowed at me. "Why? Are you looking to invest?"

"Just curious."

"$150 million ought to do it."

"Is that all?" JD asked, his voice thick with sarcasm.

Callum glared at him.

"I'll get back to my question," I said. "Did you see Eva the day you were at the Orton residence?"

Callum hesitated and shifted uncomfortably. "Why?"

"Just curious."

"You're not going to hit me with additional charges, are you?"

"Did you do something that would warrant additional charges?"

His face crinkled. "No!"

"So why are you acting sketchy?"

"I'm not acting sketchy." His eyes flicked between the two of us. "Okay, look. Yeah, I saw her that day. But I'm not some kind of creepy stalker. So get that out of your head right now."

We both looked at him, waiting for him to continue the story.

"The gate was unlocked, so I just walked into the courtyard. How can you trespass when the gate isn't locked? Anyway, I went to the front porch and knocked on the door... Nobody answered. So I walked around the side of the house to the backyard, and I saw the pool. Nice pool," he muttered aside. "Then I heard these noises, right? Like, you know..."

"What kind of noises?"

He bit his bottom lip, sneered his upper lip, made two fists, and pumped the air with his crotch like he was in a bad '70s porno. I could almost hear the bad soundtrack.

"*Those* kinds of noises," Callum said. "They were coming from the guesthouse near the pool, so I decided to *investigate*," he said in air quotes.

I frowned at him.

"Anyway, I looked through the window, not because I'm a peeper or anything. I just wanted to make sure that this was a consensual act between adults. That's when I saw Mrs. Orton bent over the kitchen counter getting pounded by some dude that wasn't Mr. Orton."

"Liam Nash," I said.

"I don't know the guy's name."

"6 foot tall, brown hair, blue eyes, good-looking?"

"Yeah, I guess. I wasn't paying attention to him, dude."

"How long did you watch?"

His eyes flicked between the two of us again. "Once I ascertained that this was a consensual act, I went about my business. I walked around the pool and peered through the windows into the living room of the main house. I didn't see anybody, so I went back around to the front of the house, and that's when Nolan and his security team arrived. They pulled into the driveway through the gate. His goons hopped out with guns drawn, shouting at me." He paused, attempting to look wounded. "I'm traumatized. I should sue him for emotional distress."

"I don't think it works that way."

"It should. I'm scarred for life."

"Have you seen Mrs. Orton since then?"

His face crinkled. "No. But I'd like to," he said with a sly grin. "What's with the questions?"

"Where were you yesterday?"

"Why?"

"Just tell us where you were between 3 and 4 PM?"

"Did something happen?"

I didn't say anything.

Panic began to wash over him. "I haven't been back to their house since that day. I swear. I haven't even tried to contact him since then, even though I think he'd be perfect for this project. I left Silicon Valley to follow the company out here."

"Sounds a little obsessive."

"I like to call it focus and determination."

"So, where were you yesterday afternoon?"

"I was here, working."

"What kind of work do you do?"

"I provide technical support over the phone to idiots who don't know how to use their computers."

"Can anyone verify your whereabouts?"

"You can check the call logs. Everything is recorded on the computer and uploaded to the system."

"You have voice recordings of all the calls?"

"Yeah, for *quality assurance*," he said in air quotes again. "Did somebody break into their home?"

"It's more serious than that."

His brow lifted with curiosity. "So, what happened?"

"You mind if we look around your apartment?"

He stammered, growing uncomfortable. "Yeah, I mind."

"I'm not gonna bust you for the weed."

"What weed?"

I gave him a look.

"Why do you want to look around my apartment?"

"To rule you out as a suspect."

His eyes widened. "I'm a suspect?"

"I can come back with a warrant," I said, knowing that we really didn't have probable cause to search for anything but weed.

"I've got nothing to hide."

"Then put your money where your mouth is."

He hesitated a moment, then stepped aside and motioned us into the apartment. "Fine. Go ahead."

We walked into the foyer and moved into the living room. There was a bong on the coffee table, a tray of weed, and a remote game controller along with a laptop and a headset. There were several entrepreneurial magazines with Nolan on the cover.

Sliding glass doors opened to a balcony that offered a stunning view of a neighboring apartment complex. There was a first-person shooter game on the 65-inch flatscreen display. The main character was stagnant, but the game continued.

"Is this your office?" I asked facetiously.

"Yeah. I just sit around and play video games all day and talk people through their tech support issues. It all comes through on the laptop, and everything is logged. He grabbed the computer, scrolled through the app, and showed us the activity from yesterday. According to the log, he was on a call from 2:42 to 3:15 PM, then again from 3:21 to 3:43 PM.

"Can I listen to these calls?"

"Just click the play icon next to the entry."

I did, and Callum's voice filtered through the laptop speakers.

That pretty much ruled him out as a suspect.

"Want to tell me what's going on?"

"Eva Orton is missing."

His brow lifted again. "Missing?"

I nodded.

He thought for a moment. "Maybe she ran off with the dude she was banging in the guest house?"

"We considered that."

We searched the rest of the apartment, checking the master bedroom, the bathroom, the closets, the guest bathroom, and a storage closet.

Eva wasn't here, and there were no kidnapping parapher-nalia—no duct tape, rope, ski masks, or any other weapons.

Callum hovered as we looked around. "We're talking about kidnapping, right?"

I nodded again.

"You don't think I had anything to do with that, do you?"

"That's why we're here to rule you out as a person of interest."

Callum swallowed hard.

13

"I can help you," Callum said. "I know everything there is to know about Nolan Orton and Flutter."

"But you're not obsessed," I said dryly.

He sneered at me. "It's called due diligence."

"If you know everything about Nolan Orton, who had a motive to kidnap his wife?"

"Duh, anybody who wanted $67 billion."

"That's tremendously helpful," I said with more than a hint of sarcasm.

"Okay. I see how it is. Dismiss my expertise. It's okay. Everyone does. But you'll see. I will soon be on top of the world, and everyone will recognize my genius."

"Modest, too," I snarked.

"You want my help or not?"

I gave him my card. "Contact me if you think of anything that might be helpful."

He studied my card for a moment. "If I give you clues that lead to the kidnappers, you think you can get the trespassing charges dropped?"

"I'm sure if you can provide information that leads to the safe recovery of Eva Orton, Nolan will be most appreciative."

Callum smiled. "Looks like I'm gonna put on my detective hat."

I forced a courteous smile.

We left the apartment and ambled down the hallway to the elevator bank. JD pressed the call button, and we waited for the lift.

"Interesting character," Jack said. "I don't think he's our guy."

"He doesn't strike me as the type, and call logs verify his whereabouts. Unless he fudged the timestamps. I don't think he has the funds to hire somebody else to kidnap her, but I could be wrong."

The bell rang, and the elevator doors slid open. We stepped aboard and plummeted down to the lobby, then made our way out to the Porsche. The sun hung high in the sky, baking the island.

I called Isabella and gave her Weston Prescott's number. She pulled up his information and tracked his phone.

"Well, he's got a good alibi."

"Do tell."

"He's not in the country. Hasn't been for a few days."

"Where's he at?"

"Monaco."

"That's a convenient excuse," I said.

"Think he could have hired somebody to do it and left town to avoid suspicion?"

"I think we're grasping at straws at this point," I said.

"I'll sift through the data and see if I can make any connections."

"Thank you. What can you tell me about Callum Anders?"

I gave her Callum's phone number. Isabella's fingers clacked against a keyboard. "Looks like his cellular device was at his apartment all day yesterday."

"What about Evan Voigt?"

Her fingers stroked the keys again. A few minutes later, she said, "This is odd. I don't see any cellular data for him yesterday afternoon. His device may have been switched off or outside of the cellular network."

I lifted an intrigued eyebrow. "We're about to track him down. I'm interested to hear what he has to say."

"If he's currently where his cell phone is, you'll find him at home in the Platinum Dunes Estates."

"Good to know. I'll be in touch. By the way, have you been able to confirm the whereabouts of Elias Fink yet?"

"I'm working on that. I'm telling you, Tyson... Be careful. Don't let your desire to get that guy cloud your judgment.

He's dangerous, and so is Sophia Breslin. Don't let her cloud your judgment either."

"I would never allow myself to be compromised like that," I said, trying to keep a straight face.

She laughed. "Anything with a short enough skirt can compromise you."

I feigned offense. "That's a cruel and unfair characterization."

"Please, save it for someone who doesn't know you better."

"She seemed like a really nice girl when I first met her," I said, trying to sound sincere.

Isabella scoffed again. "I'll talk to you later."

I ended the call, and JD cranked up the engine. We headed across the island toward the *Platinum Dunes Estates*.

My phone buzzed my pocket along the way. I snatched it and looked at the screen. Nolan's name was displayed.

I swiped an anxious thumb across the device and put the phone to my ear. "Did you hear from the kidnappers?"

14

"No, but somehow the press got hold of it, and the story is all over the news," Nolan said through a tight jaw.

I cringed.

"How did this information become public?"

"I'm not quite sure. Anybody close to the case could have leaked the information."

"This could pose a direct threat to Eva's life!"

"As I mentioned before, if they kill her, they won't get the money. Try to remain calm."

"I am calm!" he shouted. After a moment, he said, "I'm sorry. I'm just frustrated at the moment."

"I understand."

"Are you making any progress?"

"We're on our way to speak with Evan now."

"Let me know if you discover anything relevant. Keep up the good work."

"Absolutely." I ended the call, and we cruised to the ritzy neighborhood of the *Platinum Dunes*. Like *Stingray Bay*, it was an upscale neighborhood filled with McMansions and luxury cars. There was a bit of a rivalry between the two communities, each claiming more exclusivity. The *Stingray Bay* people looked down on the *Platinum Dunes* people and vice versa. If you lived in either neighborhood, you were doing pretty well.

We found Evan's place, parked at the curb, and strolled the walkway to the front door. I rang the video doorbell and pulled my badge from my pocket.

A woman's voice filtered through the speaker. "Can I help you?"

I displayed my badge to the camera. "I'm Deputy Wild with Coconut County. We'd like to speak with Evan."

She stammered, "Sure. Is there some kind of problem?"

"No problem. Just routine questions."

"Hang on a minute," she said before disconnecting. The speaker crackled.

A moment later, Evan pulled open the door. He stood about 5'10", wore a T-shirt and jeans, and had a boyish face, even though he was in his mid-30s. He had mid-length sable brown hair and brown eyes. He had a slightly nerdy quality about him. He was trim and not muscular. He didn't look like the kind of guy that could manhandle anybody.

"What can I do for you, gentlemen?" he asked with a cautious smile.

"We'd like to talk to you about your relationship with the Ortons."

"I think it's pretty clear I don't have a relationship with them."

"You owe them a great deal of restitution, don't you?"

"According to our settlement. But the terms are not supposed to be disclosed."

"Care to tell us where you were yesterday afternoon around 3 PM?"

His eyes narrowed at me. "Are you asking because of Eva's disappearance?"

"What do you know about it?"

"Only what I just saw on the news. Such a terrible thing. As much as I don't like Nolan, I hate to see anybody suffer. As a family man myself, it's deeply disturbing. And to think she was kidnapped from her home." He muttered aside. "Between you and me, that neighborhood's really gone downhill."

We stared at him blankly, giving him an opportunity to continue.

There was an awkward moment.

"To answer your question, I was here yesterday with my wife and kids. You can verify it with my wife if you desire."

"Why was your phone off the grid?"

He lifted a concerned eyebrow. "You're tracking my phone? So, I'm a person of interest?"

"Recently terminated, accused of embezzlement, you owe a substantial amount of money... I'd say, yeah, that makes you a person of interest."

A scornful chuckle burst from him. "This is just great. First of all, I didn't *embezzle* any funds," he said in air quotes. "It was a simple clerical error."

"And the funds just happened to get transferred to your personal account."

He glared at me.

"I'm not discussing this with you."

"I'm not concerned with the embezzlement at the moment. I'm just trying to find Eva."

"You're not going to find her here. He called over his shoulder, shouting down the foyer. "Honey, can you come here for a moment?"

His wife appeared in the foyer an instant later with a concerned look on her face. She was an attractive woman in her early 30s with shoulder-length wavy auburn hair. She wore a floral patterned sundress.

"Is everything okay?"

"Can you tell these gentlemen where I was yesterday?"

"Here with us. Why?"

Evan smiled at us. "See. I couldn't possibly have kidnapped Eva."

His wife's face tightened. "Evan, don't say any more to these people."

"You heard the little lady. If you have any additional questions, talk to my attorney." Evan closed the door, and that was the end of our conversation.

15

"I 'm getting the impression that not a lot of people like Nolan," JD said.

"Envy breeds contempt," I said.

We strolled the walkway to the Porsche, hopped in, and cruised across town to the warehouse district. JD had band practice.

The usual group of miscreants loitered around the entrance to the practice studio, drinking beer and smoking cigarettes. They were always out there. Pasty-faced rocker types with long jet black hair, black eyeliner, black fingernail polish, skinny jeans, and canvas hightops. I don't think these kids had jobs, but yet they always had money for beer and cigarettes.

A couple of the kids high-fived JD as we passed. As the lead singer for *Wild Fury*, JD was quickly amassing a legion of fans.

We ambled down the dim hallway that reeked of weed and spilled beer. We pushed into the practice space as the guys were tuning up. The band was gearing up for one last end of summer bash. The college kids would pack up and leave the island, heading back to school. There would typically be a little lull in tourist activity until the winter months when people fled the cold climate for the warm sunshine of the tropical paradise.

Styxx sat behind his candy-apple red drum set, and Dizzy noodled on guitar. His fingers scorched the fretboard. Crash sulked by his bass amp, his raven hair dangling in his face.

JD looked at his watch. "Let's get the show on the road. We're in the middle of a case."

I took a seat on the couch next to a couple of delightful groupies. I kept an eye on my phone in case a call from Nolan came through. I had to admit, I was starting to grow concerned with the delay. I knew the kidnappers wouldn't want to hold on to Eva any longer than they had to. They'd want to get their hands on the money as soon as possible. The longer you held a hostage, the more that could go wrong.

Yet here we were in the afternoon, 24 hours since the time of Eva's disappearance, and no ransom demand had been made.

Styxx handed JD a piece of paper with the setlist written in black sharpie. It was big enough that you could put it on the floor and still read it. "I was thinking we should play those songs for the blowout if that's okay with you?"

JD perused the list. "Fine by me."

Styxx clicked off the beat, and Dizzy and Crash thundered in on cue. A wall of sound filled the tiny practice space. JD grabbed the microphone and howled blistering rock vocals.

The groupies screamed and cheered.

As usual, curious onlookers filtered into the practice space to get a free show. The miscreants from outside popped in and out.

The small crowd always seemed to galvanize the band. What would start as a perfunctory practice would turn into a full-on performance. But today was different. Crash just went through the motions. He stood still, playing his bass guitar with his head hung low. He hardly moved around, and he didn't look like he was having fun. It brought the entire energy down.

The would-be crowd could feel it too. They clapped and cheered, but the magic was missing. It was obvious to see.

As the band's manager, it was my job to get to the bottom of it and fix the scenario. Though, I knew what the problem was without asking.

16

I pulled Crash aside after practice. We stepped into the hallway and walked away from the studio. The dull rumble of another band playing spilled into the corridor.

"What's going on with you?"

"Nothing."

"This have something to do with a particular girl?"

Crash looked up at me, peering through his jet black hair. His puffy eyes brimmed, then the dam broke. A river of tears spilled over, rolling down his cheeks. He tried to hold himself together, and he choked out the words, trying not to sob, "Faye broke up with me, man."

I frowned. "I'm sorry to hear that."

Crash wiped the tears away with the back of his hand, but they kept coming.

People had spilled out of the practice room and were loitering in the hallway now. A few of them looked in our direction, and Crash pulled himself together and stopped crying, clearly embarrassed by his display of emotion.

"It's gonna be okay."

Crash sniffled, still trying to hold it in but not doing a very good job.

"You gotta let it out. It's no good to hold it in. Give yourself a day to mourn the loss, then suck it up."

He nodded. "I know. It's just hard, man. I love her. I'm never gonna find anybody like that again. We just had that spark. It's all because of that tour. If they weren't on the road, none of this would have happened."

"Hazards of the job, my friend."

He took a deep breath, held it, then exhaled. "What am I going to do, man?"

I tried to encourage him. "Have you been paying attention? Have you been to one of our shows? Trust me, you've got plenty of options."

"Yeah, but nobody's ever going to be Faye."

"You're right. The next person will be better for you."

He didn't really want to hear anything I had to say. And none of it would make a difference anyway.

He grabbed his T-shirt collar, pulled it up, and used it to blot his eyes dry. He took another deep breath, then composed himself. Then he flexed and growled, trying to muscle through the pain. "I'm good. I swear. I'm done. That's the last time I cry. I promise."

I flashed an encouraging smile and put a comforting hand on his shoulder. "You're gonna be okay. Do the rest of the guys know?"

Crash shook his head. "They'll just dog on me when they find out and tell me how stupid I was for falling for her."

"Who cares what anybody else thinks?"

He took a moment. "You're right. It happens. We all get dumped. You get dumped, right?"

I chuckled. "I've had my share of heartbreak. No shame."

He took another deep breath, then whistled. "Whew! Okay, I'm good. I swear."

He was barely hanging on.

The rest of the guys spilled into the hallway, and JD locked up the practice space.

"Come on," he shouted. "We're going to Tide Pool."

17

I t's a rare day when JD passes up good whiskey, but with the current situation, we both wanted to stay clear-headed. That didn't keep him from buying rounds of drinks for the band, several groupies, and any other attractive females that gravitated toward the unnatural phenomenon that was *Wild Fury*.

We hung out by the outdoor pool as the sun plunged toward the horizon. There were plenty of toned bodies and taut fabric. Supple curves doused in oil, beading water. There were a lot of bars on the strip, but it was hard to beat the visual delights *Tide Pool* offered on a regular basis.

Harper kept the drinks flowing at the Tiki hut, and she had a heavy hand. I don't know how she took care of the tourists, but she never gave us watered-down drinks.

Crash took a seat at a table by the pool underneath the umbrella. He slumped in his chair and sipped a glass of whiskey. I was there if he wanted to talk about it, but if he didn't, I wasn't going to pester him anymore. I figured he'd pull out of it sooner or later. The adrenaline of being on stage would surely kick him into gear.

Faye's band, *Lip Bomb,* was touring the country, opening for various national acts, sometimes playing sold-out stadiums. It was their biggest exposure to date. They had to take the opportunity. Faye and Crash had gone through ups and downs, and it was no surprise that the rigors of the road would cause turmoil between them.

Sadie and I spared ourselves the complication and ended things before she left. We were still on good terms and talked occasionally.

I hung out, nursing a diet soda, waiting for an update on the situation. Nolan called a little after 9 o'clock. "I just heard from the kidnappers."

"And?"

"They say if I send $100 million to a Bitcoin wallet within the next 12 hours, they will release Eva unharmed."

The exorbitant demand was pocket change for Nolan. "I assume you can get your hands on that kind of money?"

"Easily."

"Did you get proof of life?"

"I asked again, but they have not replied."

"Did the message come from the same number as before?"

"Yes."

"We still don't know if these guys actually have Eva in their possession. Now that it's on the news, anybody can make ransom demands."

"Yes, but they claimed to have her before Eva's disappearance was public knowledge."

"I understand, but I'm not inclined to advise you to pay the ransom without first ascertaining proof of her well-being."

"I can appreciate that, but I just don't want to do anything that would cause Eva harm."

"We're on our way over. We'll be there in a few minutes," I said before ending the call.

I grabbed JD, and we hustled out of the bar. We jogged down the sidewalk, weaving between tourists. Music from live bands spilled into the street, and the smell of food wafted from the restaurants.

We hopped into the car, and JD cranked up the engine. He dropped it into gear and sped away from the curb. Wind swirled around the cabin with the top down.

I called Isabella. "Nolan just got another text from the kidnappers. Can you tell me about the incoming message?"

"I see the data packet that was sent to the phone, but it's encrypted. I still can't tell where it's coming from."

"Thanks. Let me know if you figure anything out."

"Good luck."

I ended the call as we twisted through the streets of *Stingray Bay*. JD pulled to the curb across from Nolan's compound, and we rushed to the pedestrian gate.

Jason buzzed us in, and a moment later, we were in the living room with Nolan, Harlow, and two additional bodyguards, John Coulter and Terrence Jamison.

Nolan paced about the living room, growing increasingly agitated. The more tense he got, the more worried Harlow looked, helpless to soothe his distress. I could tell she was highly disturbed. She was the kind of girl who prided herself on having solutions for all of Nolan's problems. It was almost like a codependent relationship. She lived through him. His satisfaction was hers.

"Why aren't they texting me back with proof of life?" Nolan growled.

"I think we have to consider the fact that they don't have her," I said.

"I don't know what to do."

"Do nothing until you hear from them," I said.

"That's easy for you to say. It's not your wife."

"No, it's not."

"We waited for another hour, and Nolan never stopped pacing. With each step, he seemed to unravel further. Finally, he said, "Fuck it. I've had enough of this."

18

Nolan launched a crypto wallet on his phone and scrolled through a few screens.

"What are you doing?" I asked, growing concerned.

"Giving them what they want." He copied and pasted the kidnapper's crypto wallet address and sent $100 million before I could stop him.

I sighed and shook my head. "You have no leverage now."

"I have a ton of leverage. I have lots more where that came from."

He sent one last text to the kidnappers that read: [I transferred the funds. Release Eva unharmed, now.]

Again we waited for a reply but received no response.

"If you're not going to take my advice, I'm not sure there's much I can do for you," I said.

"At this point, I don't think there is anything anyone can do. It's in God's hands now," he said.

I didn't figure Nolan for the religious type, but some people seem to find God in desperate times.

We hung out at his house for another hour, and still, there was no response from the kidnappers. I asked Nolan if he wanted us to stay at the house for the rest of the night in case they responded.

"That won't be necessary. I have ample security. If anything arises, I will contact you."

"Anytime, day or night. We're here. Don't hesitate to call."

"I can't thank you enough for everything you've done. I just hope these people do the right thing and let Eva go."

I tried to remain optimistic. Counting on criminals to do the right thing rarely worked out.

We left Nolan's and drove back to *Diver Down*. We stopped at the bar for a drink. Alejandro was serving. Teagan had long since gotten off for the evening. He poured a couple glasses of whiskey and slid them across the counter.

We sipped our drinks and tried to unwind. But there was nothing to celebrate about this day.

"Think Eva is still alive?" JD asked.

"The lack of proof of life is worrisome."

"I think... Well, I'm not gonna say what I think." Jack took another sip.

We hung out and finished our drink. It was late, and we were both tired. JD headed home, and I ambled down the dock to the *Avventura*.

Despite the grim outlook, my hope was that Eva was still alive. With any luck, she'd turn up by the morning, having been released somewhere.

But I wasn't holding my breath.

The moon cast a glow over the marina, and the boats gently swayed in their slips. It was a calm evening. I crossed the passerelle to the aft deck, and Buddy greeted me when I slid open the salon door.

Sophia Breslin sat on the settee, sipping a glass of whiskey. "I think he's taken a liking to me."

My eyes narrowed at her, and my face crinkled.

Buddy trotted back to the settee, jumped up, and curled beside her. She stroked his fur with a small grin on her face.

Traitor.

She wore a tight black dress and stilettos. Her long, sumptuous legs drew the eye.

"What are you doing here, and how did you get in?"

She scoffed. "Please. There is no lock that can resist my charm."

She grabbed a manila envelope and tossed it on the hi-lo table.

"What's this?" I asked, snapping up the envelope.

"What you asked for."

I unclasped the folder and pulled out the contents. There were several pictures of Elias Fink eating at a sidewalk café in Caracas. The images had been taken with an extremely long telephoto lens. There were close-ups and wide-angles. It was clearly the infamous terrorist.

"How do I know these are recent?"

"Look at the date on the billboard in the wide-angle shot."

I studied the image of the bustling city street filled with cars and pedestrians. Buses and mid-rise buildings. Weeds sprouted from the medians and looked like they hadn't been tended to in ages. Nature was attempting to reclaim the urban sprawl that was in decay due to the economic and political turmoil.

There was a vertical billboard on the side of a building advertising a Latin pop music star with the dates of her upcoming show a week from today. "How do I know this wasn't manipulated?"

Sophia rolled her eyes. "You're going to have to trust me at some point."

"Trust, but verify. Send me the original digital images, if you have them."

She grabbed her phone, and her svelte fingers danced across the keyboard, clicking and clacking. She sent a handful of images that buzzed my device a moment later. I forwarded them to Isabella. She could analyze them for authenticity and digital manipulation.

"How did you get these?"

Sophia smiled. "I have a source. And my source followed him back to an apartment. I have the address, if you want it."

"I do."

She texted it to me, and again I forwarded it to Isabella.

"Time is of the essence," Sophia said. "He might not be there for long. We need to move fast."

"I need confirmation first."

"And once you get it, then we'll go down and kill him?"

"That will be up for discussion."

She smiled. "At least that's a start."

She pressed her full lips against the glass and finished the last of the whiskey. She held it out to me and wiggled the glass, demanding more.

I stood there for a moment, glaring at her.

She arched her eyebrow and wiggled her glass again. "Where are your manners? You should be thanking me. I'm bringing you valuable information."

I sighed and stepped forward, taking the glass from her hand. Our fingers touched for an instant.

I moved to the bar and poured us both a drink, then returned and handed her a full glass. She lifted it to toast. "To taking care of our problem."

I reluctantly clinked glasses. We both sipped our beverages.

"You know, that's one thing I like about you—you don't drink cheap whiskey."

"It's the simple pleasures," I said.

A naughty sparkle flickered her eyes. "Speaking of pleasure. How about we consummate our new partnership? For old time's sake."

"As I recall, last time I ended up in bed with you, you tried to kill me."

"At least you had a good time."

My eyes narrowed at her. "And you killed my friend, Quinn. The only reason you're not dead right now is because—"

"Because I saved your ass, and you need me."

I frowned at her.

"And you want me. You can't deny it." She arched her torso, showing off her luscious endowments.

They were compelling features.

"Finish your drink and go before I decide to arrest you or worse."

She made a pouty face. "You don't really want me to go, do you?"

"Yes, I do. I'd like to get a good night's sleep."

"Who needs sleep?"

I continued to scowl at her.

"What if I told you I didn't kill Quinn Palmer."

"Liar."

"I'm not lying."

I rolled my eyes.

"Elias hired multiple hitters. Someone else got there first. I tried to take credit. Sue me."

"A likely story."

"Think about how Quinn's boyfriend was killed. He was hanging from a noose when they found him. You think I really had the strength to hoist him up on the rafters all by myself?"

"And what about the shots you took at me in the hospital parking lot?"

She gave a quick shrug. "Okay, that was me. But I missed, didn't I?"

I sneered at her.

"How about we start over? I'm sorry I tried to kill you. I promise I won't do it again. What can I do to make it up to you?"

I trusted Sophia Breslin about as far as I could throw her. I figured I could manage to throw her overboard, and that was about it. I probably should have done it.

"If you didn't kill Quinn Palmer, who did?"

"I got myself into the hotel room next door. I climbed across the balcony to her room, and she was already dead. I swear. Elias's other hitter had gotten there first, just like with the other targets. It was starting to piss me off. So, I started tracking him. Sometimes the hunters forget they can also be hunted."

"Are you trying to tell me you hit the hitman?"

"I'm not stupid enough to admit to a deputy that I killed someone. So I'm not going to say that. But if you need proof of death, I might be able to tell you where you could find the remains."

"How convenient."

"It's part of the reason Elias is so pissed off at me. Not only did I botch the job of killing you, I... Well, you get the picture."

"Where can I find the remains of said hitman?"

19

"W hy?" Sophia asked. "So you can arrest me?"

"I think I've already got enough reason to arrest you," I replied.

"And yet you haven't," she said with a sassy eyebrow.

"The night is young."

She laughed.

"You should leave before I change my mind."

She took another swig from her glass, draining the last of the whiskey. She set it down on the table, then stood up and sauntered toward me like a jungle cat stalking her prey. Her hungry eyes were locked onto mine. She stepped close and whispered in a velvety voice, "I'm not as bad as you think I am."

Her lips hovered inches from mine.

"Yes, you are."

She smirked and pushed away from me, heading toward the salon door. "Good night, Deputy Wild."

Buddy followed her to the door, and I held onto his collar so he didn't dart out.

"Bye, Buddy," she said.

He barked.

Sophia blew me a kiss and strode across the aft deck to the passerelle, her high heels clacking.

"I want my tender back," I shouted.

She ignored me.

I slid the salon door shut and locked it—not that it would keep her out. I just shook my head as I watched her strut down the dock.

I looked at Buddy in dismay. "How could you?"

He looked up at me with sad, pathetic eyes, tilted his head, and whimpered slightly.

"I know, I know. She does have a certain *quality*."

He barked again.

I climbed up to the bridge deck and stepped into my stateroom. I settled into bed for the evening and woke with the sunrise, amber shafts blasting in.

I yawned and stretched and wiped the sleep from my eyes. Then grabbed the phone from the nightstand. There was no message from Isabella. No call from Nolan. Nothing.

I got up, fixed breakfast, and took Buddy out for a walk. When I returned to the *Avventura,* I finally got a call with the bad news.

"They haven't let her go," Nolan said. "There has been no contact from them, despite my repeated attempts at communication. I've been up all night. Have your people discovered anything?"

"Unfortunately, no. But every agency is looking."

"She's dead, isn't she?" he said, his voice quivering.

"Let's not jump to any conclusions yet."

"Why else wouldn't they respond?"

"We still have to consider the possibility that they never had Eva in their possession."

"Then where is she?"

"Maybe she was seeing someone else besides Liam. Maybe she ran off."

Nolan was silent for a moment.

"I'm not going to sugarcoat things," I said. "Something could have gone wrong. She could very well be dead. But until we know that for certain, we need to hold onto hope."

"I don't have much of that at this point."

"I understand. It's possible she has been released in a remote location and doesn't have access to a phone."

"What if Liam killed her? What if she broke it off with him like I asked her to do? Maybe he got mad. Maybe he killed her because he couldn't be with her."

"I don't think we can rule anything out yet. We will continue to pursue all avenues."

"I know you're doing your best."

"Is there anyone else you can think of that we should be looking into?"

"I'm going to put you in touch with Natalie Conroy. She's the head of our Trust and Security team for the platform. She would be aware of all of the online threats."

"She would have been a handy person to talk to sooner."

"I'm sorry. In all the chaos, I wasn't thinking clearly. She's the one who coordinates the threat reports and sends them to the security detail. I'll send you her contact info."

He did so after hanging up.

I called Natalie Conroy and introduced myself.

"Deputy Wild, thanks for getting in touch. Nolan said you would be contacting me."

"I wish I would have talked to you sooner."

"Agreed. Sometimes Nolan is a little scatterbrained. And I can't imagine the stress he's under currently."

"Have there been any online communications or threats that you think could correlate to Eva's kidnapping."

"We get more online threats than you could possibly imagine, and more than Nolan knows about."

"You keep information from him?"

"No. We minimize the amount of noise that he has to deal with to keep his bandwidth manageable."

"So, you are vetting and discarding low-level threats."

"Yes. The ones we think are credible, we refer to the security detail. They vet them even further. Nolan doesn't need to spend his time worrying about things that should be the focus of the security detail. Nolan's focus is to steer the ship so that we all move in the right direction."

"Does anything stand out?"

"We've received thousands of threats. We deplatform users for incorrect speech."

"Incorrect?"

"Offensive. As you can imagine, that makes some people quite angry."

"I would imagine so."

"We've gotten bomb threats at the office. Vandals have broken windows. Cars have been damaged in the parking lot, and property has been defaced with spray paint."

"You're a global platform. What about terrorist organizations and cartels?"

"We have advanced detection algorithms that scan private message content for potentially illegal activity—child pornography, drug trafficking, terrorist activity. If the algorithm flags something, it is reviewed by an actual person and brought to a safety committee. From there, we make a decision on whether or not to notify law enforcement."

"What about user privacy?"

"There is a balance between privacy and security."

"Have you made any recent reports to law enforcement?"

20

"I gave this information to Liam several months ago," Natalie said. "Was this not given to you?"

"Liam is no longer part of the team," I said.

"I know, but I assumed Jason would have been aware. We turned over the private messages that led to the arrest and conviction of 15 members of the Falcon Syndicate including the head of the organization, Felix Ramos. I believe the arrests took place in Pineapple Bay in coordination with local law enforcement and the DEA."

"I remember hearing something about that, but it wasn't made public that Flutter cooperated with law enforcement," I said.

"We like to keep those details out of the press. As you can imagine, it undermines user confidence."

"I would imagine so. Are there any other similar incidents I should be aware of?"

"That's the most recent and most notable. I can send you a summary of all our threat assessments over the last six months."

"That would be extremely helpful."

I gave her my email address and thanked her for the information. I ended the call and dialed Isabella. "What can you tell me about Felix Ramos and the Falcon Syndicate?"

Her fingers danced across the keyboard. "Real nice guys. Drug trafficking, human trafficking, kidnapping, extortion, racketeering... Should I go on?"

"I think I get the picture."

"Felix Ramos is currently serving a life sentence, as are several other members of the organization. According to my information, Felix's son, Javier, has taken over the syndicate. You think this has something to do with the Orton kidnapping?"

"Seeing how the people at *Flutter* notified law enforcement of the gang's activity, I'd say Eva's kidnapping could be motivated by revenge."

"Felix is currently in a holding pod at the Pineapple Bay Detention Center awaiting transfer to the state penitentiary," Isabella said. Her fingers tapped the keys again. "Javier lives on a boat in *Pirates' Cove*. I'll see if he's got a cell phone that's trackable."

"Let me know what you find out."

"I will."

"Were you able to determine the authenticity of the photos I sent you?"

"They don't appear to be manipulated. I'm trying to get eyes on Elias for confirmation. I'll let you know as soon as I hear something."

I ended the call and rang JD. I filled him in on the situation.

"What do you want to do?"

"I don't want to tip Javier off," I said. "If he has kidnapped Eva and we go snooping around, that might spell bad news for her."

"I've got bad news for you. I think she's dead already. I think something went wrong. Maybe one of the captors got a little aggressive, who knows?"

"Let's try to stay positive," I said. "I've got Isabella trying to track his phone. With any luck, she can intercept his calls. In the meantime, I say we go over in the surveillance van and see what we can find out."

"You know how much I love a stakeout," JD said, his voice dripping with sarcasm.

I told him I'd meet him at the station. I grabbed my helmet and gloves and hustled down the dock to the parking lot. I straddled my bike and cranked up the engine, twisting the throttle a few times. The exhaust growled a sweet note.

I eased out the clutch and rolled out of the parking lot. When I turned on the highway, I let her rip, running through the gears.

The sportbike was pure exhilaration. It was a top-of-the-line, 1000cc crotch rocket. It was one step removed from a MotoGP bike. Blistering speed and superb handling.

I hugged the tank, and the wind whistled my ears as I blazed down the road at more than twice the legal limit.

I had a get out of jail free card, and I abused it from time to time.

A few moments later, I pulled into the parking lot at the station. JD joined me in his Miami Blue Porsche not long after.

The surveillance van was still wrapped to look like a plumbing company—*Dr. Drippy's Pipe and Drain*. We updated the disguise with a new vinyl wrap from time to time. Nobody ever pays attention to maintenance vehicles.

We recruited one of the tech guys for the mission. Crenshaw was always eager to get out of the office and into the field. He'd gone on a few of our stakeouts before and had gotten a taste for the intelligence-gathering aspect of it. He was a good guy but was well versed in all the hacker tricks.

We all hopped into the van, drove over to *Pirates' Cove,* and parked in the lot. I climbed into the back with JD and Crenshaw.

There were large flatscreen displays, and the van was outfitted with a high-definition camera and a slew of surveillance toys.

"So what's the plan?" Crenshaw asked.

irates' Cove was filled with sport-fishing boats, small sailboats, speedboats, and a few motor yachts. Some were on the larger side, but you didn't see a lot of 140-footers here. It was a mid-level marina that lacked the upkeep and amenities of the more prestigious locations.

From our location in the van, we had a line of sight on Javier's boat, *The Bandit*. Probably not the smartest thing for a gangster to name his boat. It was an older 45-foot sport-fish. A nice boat but not too flashy for a gangster. He was trying to fly under the radar, living in *Pirate's Cove*. But he wasn't doing a good job of it, sending mixed signals with the boat's moniker.

"I need ears on that boat," I said.

"So, you want me to do illegal shit?" Crenshaw asked, almost eagerly. A sly grin tugged his lips.

"We need to find out if he's got any involvement in the kidnapping," JD said. "If he doesn't, we move on."

A call from Isabella interrupted the discussion. "Looks like Javier has gotten smart. He doesn't have a cell phone in his name."

"If I get you his position, can you triangulate a burner phone in the same location?"

"If it's turned on."

"Ok, hang on." I slid open the door to the van and stepped out. "Can you track my phone?"

I heard her fingers run across the keyboard. "Ok, I've got you."

I pulled the door shut and walked across the lot with the phone to my ear. I casually strolled the dock until I was standing in front of *The Bandit*.

"It's just in front of me to the north. I'm 5 feet from the stern."

I kept walking so it wouldn't be too obvious. From my reference point, Isabella was able to calculate the GPS coordinates of the boat. She could then look for devices that were pinging the cell tower at that position.

A lot of people buy prepaid cellular phones, thinking they are anonymous. But then they go home and make phone calls. The GPS data is relayed to the cell tower. It doesn't take a rocket scientist to put two and two together when law enforcement is monitoring a particular suspect. Wireless devices tend to connect automatically to local networks. Perps often use their prepaid cellular connected to their home wireless network, once again compromising their identity. If you want to stay truly anonymous in the digital age, you have to go to great lengths, and it's easy to slip up. All it takes is one mistake to compromise your identity.

I continued down the dock, trying to look inconspicuous. After a moment of looking out over the harbor, I turned around and headed back to the parking lot. I gave a glance around, making sure no one was paying attention, then I pulled open the door to the van and stepped back inside, still on the phone with Isabella.

"I'm not picking up any cellular devices aboard *The Bandit*," she said. "If Javier's got a burner phone, it's turned off. I'll let you know if anything pops up," she said before ending the call.

"We can try to hack his wireless network like we did those other thugs," Crenshaw said.

"It's worth a shot," I replied.

Crenshaw dug into his backpack and pulled out a small device that looked like a portable game.

"What's that?" JD asked.

"A wireless network sniffer. If he's got a wireless network onboard, it will give me information about signal strength, security protocols, and vulnerabilities."

Crenshaw moved to the door and slid it open.

"What are you going to do?"

"Walk down the dock, sniff the network information, then come back."

"Don't be too obvious about it," I warned.

His face crinkled. "Relax. This isn't my first rodeo."

He hopped out and slid the door shut behind him.

Crenshaw had come a long way from that kid who was freaked out about planting a bug in a tattoo parlor. Now he was more than eager to take an active role in our surveillance shenanigans.

JD sat behind the control terminal and adjusted the cameras on the van with a joystick. He guided the high-definition camera and long-range mic to follow Crenshaw as he walked down the dock.

Crenshaw held the device in his hand and strolled to *The Bandit*. He stood there a moment, looking at the device.

That's when Javier stepped out of the salon. His brow knitted together. "What the fuck are you doing?"

22

J D and I watched the monitor and cringed. A long range microphone aimed toward the dock filtered audio through the speakers.

Crenshaw maintained his cool. He spoke in a slow, lazy voice, like a stoned surfer. He squinted his eyes, playing the part. "I'm looking for my buddy's boat, the *Barnacle*. This ain't it."

"No shit."

Javier was mid 20s with short dark hair and brown eyes. He was probably about 5'9" and had a medium build.

Crenshaw frowned and glanced around. "This is Sandpiper Point, right?"

"No, dipshit. This is Pirates' Cove."

"No way!"

"Yes, way."

Crenshaw casually slipped the device into his pocket. He looked around again, then leaned in and spoke in a hushed tone. "You don't know where I can score some weed, do you?"

Javier's face tensed with annoyance. "No, bro," he said, mocking him. "I don't know where you can score weed."

"Right on, man. No problem."

Crenshaw spun around and walked back down the dock toward the parking lot. He pulled out his phone and pretended to call a friend. "Bro, I'm at Pirates' Cove." He continued to have a conversation with himself. "Fuck off, I'm not high..."

Javier watched him for a moment, then stepped back into the salon.

Crenshaw meandered around for a while, and when it was clear he wasn't being watched, he returned to the van.

"What did you find out?" I asked.

"Slow your roll," he said.

Crenshaw pulled a laptop from his backpack, flipped open the screen, and launched an app that was a favorite of hackers worldwide. Having learned Javier's network ID with the help of the sniffer, Crenshaw was able to make additional tests to the network from his laptop. "He's using a robust security protocol with an extended passphrase. I'm not going to be able to crack that with brute force. There are no IOT devices on his network that can be easily hacked and no smart TVs."

"Looks like he's no dummy," JD said.

"Sorry guys. You're gonna have to do this the old-fashioned way."

JD frowned. "I'm not real keen on sitting around in this van for a few hours."

"We might not have to," I said, nodding to the video monitor.

Javier stepped from the salon, crossed the cockpit, pushed through the transom door, and hopped to the dock. He had a black duffel bag in his hand, and it looked pretty heavy.

JD fiddled with the joystick, following him along with the camera.

Javier made his way to the parking lot, threw the duffel bag into the trunk of a late-model fire-engine red Camaro, then hopped behind the wheel. He cranked up the engine, and the exhaust rumbled. He cruised out of the parking lot, and I slid behind the wheel of the van and started her up.

We followed him onto the highway and hung back a reasonable distance. Maybe we'd get lucky and he'd lead us to Eva if she was still alive.

It was a big *if*.

Javier drove north, heading out of town. We put a few cars between the plumbing van and his Camaro as we followed along.

Javier cruised past the *Pink Pussycat,* past the *Seahorse Shores* motel. We followed him all the way up to Pineapple Bay.

He made a few twists and turns through the city, and I worried that our plumbing van might start to look suspicious.

Javier pulled into a self-serve car wash and drove into an empty stall.

It was a long way to go for a car wash, especially when there was one just like it in Coconut Key.

He hopped out of the Camaro, put change in the machine, and started hosing down his ride.

We parked the van across the street, and JD angled the cameras toward the car wash.

"What do you think this is about?" JD asked.

I shrugged.

We'd find out soon enough.

A blue Honda four-door pulled into the stall next to Javier. A burly dude got out, walked around the back of his car, and made his way to Javier. He was a big guy—6'2", 250 lbs. Bald with a bit of a belly.

"Record this," I said to JD.

He fumbled to activate the recording. Crenshaw nudged him out of the way since he was occupying the seat at the control center. Crenshaw took his place and started recording the high-def footage.

We were in a public place, and they were in plain view. We didn't need a warrant for this. Whatever we recorded would be admissible. They had no expectation of privacy in a public car wash.

Javier clicked his key fob and popped the trunk. The lid lifted by itself, and the burly dude strode to the trunk, grabbed the duffel bag, then returned to his car.

The two didn't say a word.

The burly guy threw the bag in the trunk, hopped behind the wheel, and drove away.

I made a note of the burly dude's plate and texted it to Denise at the station. [Can you tell me who owns this vehicle?]

I gave her a description of the guy and the car.

"What do you think was in the bag?" Crenshaw asked.

"Drugs, guns, or cash," JD said.

Denise called me a moment later. "The car is registered to Edward Collins. He works for the county. He's a transportation officer at the Pineapple Bay Detention Center."

I lifted a surprised brow. "Really?"

"What's going on?"

"I don't know for sure, but I've got a pretty good idea. See if you can find out the transportation schedule for Felix Ramos. Something tells me Javier Ramos just bribed Ed Collins."

Denise's fingers danced across the keyboard. A moment later, she said, "Felix is scheduled to be transferred from Pineapple Bay to the Everglades Correctional Institution."

"When?"

"Tomorrow."

That hung there for a moment.

"Is the sheriff around? I need to talk to him right away."

"Yeah. I'll transfer you to his desk."

The sheriff's gruff voice filtered through the speaker, and I updated him on the situation. He grumbled under his breath. "That city is so corrupt."

We had our fair share of corruption in Coconut Key, but Pineapple Bay took things to another level. There were so many officials on the take, from judges to city councilman to officers on the street.

"I can call Captain Jefferson at the Pineapple Bay substation and notify him of the situation."

I hesitated. "At this point, how do we know he's not involved?"

"You're going out on a limb, aren't you?"

"Javier handed a county officer a duffel bag the day before his father is scheduled to be transported. Doesn't take a rocket scientist to figure out what's going down."

"I'm playing devil's advocate here, but you have no idea what was in that bag."

"I don't need to know. We just need to stop this thing from happening and arrest everyone involved. It's Pineapple Bay after all."

Daniels grunted.

"I say we put together a tac team and wait for this to go down. There's no telling how many people are involved."

"How do you see this thing playing out?"

"Ed Collins probably will give Javier the time and route. He's the only officer scheduled, and Felix is the only passenger. He'll just let it happen. Javier and his thugs will block off the vehicle and force the release of his father at gunpoint. Ed won't resist. When it's all over, Ed will have plausible deniability, and Felix Ramos will be a fugitive."

"And how does this tie into the Orton kidnapping?"

"Maybe it does, maybe it doesn't. But right now, we've got a duty to stop it. Pineapple Bay is within Coconut County. It's our jurisdiction."

Daniels was silent for a moment. "Alright. Put together a tac team, and don't screw this up."

24

We headed back to Coconut Key, and by the time we arrived, we were all starving. We took Crenshaw for a bite to eat at *Juicy Burger*. We chowed on greasy cheeseburgers and fries before heading back to the station.

The office bustled with activity. Phones rang, and deputies processed perps and handled complaints. We found Denise at her desk amid the chaos.

"The transfer is happening at 10 AM tomorrow," she said. "I notified Erickson, Faulkner, Robinson, and Mendoza. I figured you'd want them on the team."

I nodded. "Nice work."

The gorgeous redhead smiled, flashing her perfect teeth. Her emerald eyes sparkled. "What would you do without me?"

"My world would end," I said, not lying.

"I've notified the helicopter unit. *Tango One* will provide air support."

"I want to go," Crenshaw added.

"You are not a field officer. You're not even a deputy."

"That's what you said last time."

"We got shot at last time."

"I just want to ride along and observe. You need technical support on this."

I gave him a doubtful glance.

"Come on, do me a solid."

"Ask the sheriff."

Crenshaw's face crinkled. "He's gonna say *'No'*."

Crenshaw looked across the busy room to the sheriff's office. Daniels was on the phone.

"Go ahead," I taunted. "Just walk right in there and demand that you be included on this."

Crenshaw shrank, and he squeaked, "He doesn't look too receptive at the moment."

"He never looks receptive."

"Any word on Eva Orton?" Denise asked.

I shook my head.

JD made a grim face.

Denise cringed. "That's not good, is it?"

"No, it's not."

I called Nolan to touch base, and he still hadn't heard anything from the kidnappers. "How long should I give it before I assume the worst? I mean, I'm already assuming the worst, but... I guess what I'm asking is, when does this turn from a kidnapping into a homicide investigation in your eyes?"

Nolan's voice sounded thin and scratchy. The voice of a man pushed to the edge, terrified and exhausted. I figured he hadn't slept much in the last few days. I know I wouldn't be able to close my eyes if I were in his shoes.

"Right now, we are still investigating this case as a kidnapping until we have reason to believe otherwise."

"I've got tech people trying to track down that crypto wallet and see if they can connect it to an individual."

"My people are working on that as well," I said.

"If you learn anything, let me know."

"You'll be my first call," I assured.

I ended the call and slipped the phone into my pocket.

Denise frowned. "I feel so bad for that man."

We all did.

I said goodbye to Denise and left the station with JD. I hopped on my bike, and he followed me back to the marina at *Diver Down*. We stopped at the bar and took a seat at the counter.

"Two whiskeys?" Teagan asked.

"You read my mind," JD said

Teagan smiled. "I'm good like that."

Paris Delaney was on the flatscreen behind the bar. She, and a gaggle of other vultures, were huddled outside Nolan Orton's home, hoping to catch a glimpse of the beleaguered billionaire. They were all speculating on the fate of Eva Orton. It was a ratings boon, and there was almost constant coverage on every news channel.

Isabella called. "Well, your girlfriend isn't entirely wrong. But she's not entirely right."

"Fink is gone?"

"My sources tell me he was there, but he's not now."

"Those photos were recent," I said.

"Not recent enough. Something could have spooked him. He left within the last day or so. Do you know where she's getting her intel?"

"I don't. Do you think he's still in Venezuela?"

"That's what I'm trying to figure out. The guy is good. He's managed to elude captivity for the last decade. We've gotten close a number of times before, but he always manages to slip away."

"Keep on it."

"You know that I will. And be careful. I don't have to tell you that, but I feel compelled to."

"It's nice that you care," I snarked.

"I do care. I don't want to see one of my best operatives harmed," Isabella said. "And Sophia's already taken out a few."

"She actually denies responsibility for that."

"Of course she does. Would you expect anything less from her? She is a snake."

"I take everything she says with a grain of salt."

"Good. Don't let her bamboozle you. She is, and always will be, a killer."

I ended the call and told JD that Elias Fink had moved on.

"You need to quit associating with that crazy-ass."

"I'm not associating with her. I'm using her for intel."

"Stale intel that is of no tactical value."

Just at that moment, a call from Sophia Breslin buzzed through on an encrypted messaging app. I showed the screen to JD. "Speak of the devil."

He frowned and shook his head as I swiped the screen.

"Miss me?"

"Your intel was wrong," I said.

"I know, I just found out. That's why I'm calling you and giving you a heads up so you don't think I'm full of shit."

"I already think you're full of shit."

"I'm sorry you feel that way."

"Call it self-preservation."

"You've built up too many walls, Tyson."

I chuckled. "You are the last person I need to lower the shields for."

"I'm telling you, we're on the same team now. What do I have to do to convince you?"

"I'm not sure that you can."

"Holden Cauley."

"Who?"

"The hitman that killed Quinn. His name is... *was*... Holden Cauley. Look him up."

"I will."

25

I texted Isabella the hitman's name and asked her to see what she could find out.

The next morning I suited up in tactical gear with a bulletproof vest and extra magazines. JD swung by the marina in the Porsche, and we cruised up to the station to meet with the rest of the team. We had a tactical briefing in the conference room before heading up to Pineapple Bay.

The guys from the helicopter unit were in attendance, along with Crenshaw. He had a wide smile on his face and eager eyes. I wondered what the hell he was doing there. Daniels didn't seem to mind his presence, so I figured he'd gotten the A-OK. It was unusual for Daniels to make any kind of concessions.

I went over the plan with the team. We'd stake out the detention center and follow the transport when it left. *Tango One* would be in the air, giving us constant updates about our surroundings and incoming threats. We'd follow along in the Porsche, and the other deputies would be in unmarked vehicles. If something went down, we'd thwart their efforts.

It all sounded good in theory. But no plan ever survives the battlefield.

I used a projector to display images of Ed Collins, Javier Ramos, and maps of predicted routes. I discussed possible methods of attack the thugs might use.

"Does anybody have any questions?" I asked after my briefing.

"Yeah," Faulkner said. "Who's buying the beer afterward?"

Everybody chuckled.

I pointed to JD.

"If this goes down clean and without a hitch, I'm buying," Sheriff Daniels said.

We all gave him a surprised glance.

"Let's get it done quickly and without incident. I don't want this turning into a debacle out on the streets. If it goes south, somebody will catch it on a cell phone, and it will be all over the internet by noon."

We filed out of the conference room, and I asked Crenshaw, "Did Daniels approve this?"

"He said I can ride in Tango One!" He could barely contain himself.

"I figure he's safe up there as long as the rotor blades keep turning," Daniels said, bringing up the rear.

We all hustled out of the station. JD and I hopped into the Porsche and pulled out of the parking lot, heading north. He kept it at a reasonable speed as we caravanned up to Pineapple Bay. The two unmarked units trailed behind us. The plain white vehicles stuck out like sore thumbs, and it only took a quick glance to realize they were county vehicles.

JD blasted the stereo on the way up, and the wind swooshed about the cabin. The morning sun beamed down, and the Porsche's engine growled.

It wasn't long before we cruised into Pineapple Bay. We twisted our way through the streets toward the substation. We pulled into the parking lot of an apartment complex across from the detention center. It was lined with palm trees and bushes. A row of hedges separated it from the roadway. It provided a reasonable amount of cover.

Similar to Coconut Key, the detention center consisted of several housing pods to contain inmates of various threat levels. The area was surrounded by a chain-link fence that was rimmed with concertina wire. Green and gold signs demarcated it as county property, and red and white warning signs told people to keep out.

There were plenty of county vehicles parked in the lot inside the fence—unmarked patrol units, vans, and personal vehicles. The facility was nestled near the eastern shore, and the apartment complex across the street backed up to a large marina.

We had a line of sight to the detention center and had a clear view of the departure zone. The county had strict protocols when it came to prisoner transports. How closely those protocols would be followed was another story.

Inmates were to be searched for weapons and contraband before any transportation, and the transport vehicle was to be searched before and after. Much like a preflight check before take-off, each vehicle was to be examined for safety and functionality. You didn't want to get out on the road without a spare tire, tire jack, and a lug wrench. All units were required to carry reflective triangles or cones and a first aid kit. Tires were inflated to proper pressure along with a full fuel tank and sufficient oil.

Once a prisoner was in motion, the transportation officer's sole function was to deliver the inmate to the destination. They weren't supposed to stop and render aid, or interfere with the commission of a crime, or do anything else that could compromise the security of the inmate. In those situations, they were required to call for backup and keep moving. The only exception to that rule was if two deputies were present during the transport, and one could remain with the prisoner at all times.

There were rules about bathroom breaks and modifications to the vehicles. The protocols dictated if and when they could stop for meals. The deputy would choose the restaurant and the prisoner's food. Inmates weren't allowed to order for themselves. It wouldn't be hard to smuggle a knife into a chili dog.

I watched through binoculars, waiting for any sign of the transport vehicle or Ed Collins. We'd been sitting there for half an hour with no indication of activity. I looked at my watch, and it was just after 10 AM. After another 15 minutes waiting, I called Denise to make sure everything was still on schedule. She pulled the information up on the computer. "As far as I can tell, nothing's been changed."

It was almost 10:30 when Ed pulled the transportation van around to the departure zone. It was a large white van with the green and gold logo of the Sheriff's Department on the side.

Ed hopped out and walked around the vehicle, checking the tires and doing a quick visual inspection. He opened the back double doors. Inside the cargo area was a metal cage that housed inmates during transport. Once inside, prisoners wouldn't have any access to windows or the driver. They could be passed food and other items through access slots.

Ed unlocked the cage and swung the door wide, then waited by the vehicle.

A few moments later, another deputy escorted Felix out of the detention center. He shuffled across the lot, wearing an orange jumpsuit, shackled around the wrists and ankles.

Felix was in his late 50s. His charcoal hair was graying on the sides, and there was gray in his mustache. He looked small compared to Ed. Felix probably stood about 5'8". He had a medium build and looked fit. If he wasn't in orange, he'd look like your neighbor. Friendly and harmless. Not the head of a ruthless organization.

Ed searched the prisoner for weapons and contraband, patting him down. He helped Felix into the van and locked him in the cage.

Ed signed off on the paperwork, taking custody of the prisoner, then walked around the van, hopped behind the wheel, and cranked up the engine.

The razor-wire gate slid open, and the van rolled out of the facility.

The show was about to begin.

26

Tango One hovered high in the sky, the rotor blades pattering overhead. The helicopter hung back, trying not to be too conspicuous. We followed the van from the detention center, twisting through the streets of Pineapple Bay to the main highway.

I kept a vigilant watch, my eyes scanning in all directions. The Miami Blue Porsche stuck out like a sore thumb, but a corrupt transportation officer wouldn't likely suspect two deputies to be in a high-end sports car. I was much more worried about the trail of unmarked vehicles behind us.

Ed turned the van north onto the highway, and we followed him out of town.

So far, no sign of any threats.

There were a few cars between us and the van as we headed north. The highway was two lanes in each direction at this point.

We cruised over the water, and at the next small key, the highway narrowed to one lane in either direction, separated by a solid double yellow line.

In this particular area, there was a shoulder, a small bit of gravel, some grass and shrubs, then marshy water.

I waited anxiously for an enemy strike.

It wasn't long before a vehicle came up on us at a high rate of speed. It veered across the double yellow lines when the oncoming traffic was clear and soared past us. I thought this might be it.

The vehicle continued past our convoy and zipped in behind the transport van. At the next break in traffic, it crossed the double yellow line again, passed the van, then pulled back into the lane in front of the transport.

Nothing happened for another minute or two.

Then three more cars came up fast behind us, crossing the double yellows. They streaked by at over 100 miles an hour, the turbulent wind buffeting the car, rocking the chassis from side to side.

This was it. I was sure of it.

One vehicle pulled alongside the van as the car in front of it slowed. Another vehicle veered onto the shoulder on the right side of the van, boxing it in, and the fourth vehicle blocked the rear.

With textbook precision, they forced the van to the shoulder of the road and came to a stop, blocking the outgoing lane of traffic completely.

The two uninvolved cars in front of us stopped. JD veered onto the shoulder, passing them, pulling up to the scene.

Masked thugs hopped out of the vehicles blocking the van and surrounded the transport. They all wielded black assault rifles. The leader of the group shouted at Ed to step out of the vehicle, his angry weapon aimed at the crooked deputy.

Ed raised his hands in the air and stepped out of the vehicle into the roadway.

The gang leader marched him to the rear of the van, and Ed unlocked the doors, then unlocked the cage.

I hopped out of the Porsche, taking cover behind the open door. The rest of our squad swooped in behind me.

"Freeze!" I yelled. "Coconut County. Drop the weapons!"

My demand didn't go over too well.

The thugs aimed their assault rifles at me and opened fire. Clattering gunfire echoed, muzzle flash flickered, and smoke wafted from barrels.

I ducked for cover behind the door as bullets webbed the windshield with cracks and pelted the hood and door panels. The impacts popped and pinged. Shards of glass sprinkled.

JD crouched below the dashboard as bullets rocketed through the air.

Maybe this wasn't such a good idea.

The other deputies returned fire.

I angled my pistol over the top of the door, found a target, and squeezed the trigger. The pistol hammered against my palm, and gunpowder filled my nostrils. The deafening ruckus rang my ears.

It was pure chaos.

Bullets crossed the air.

Blood-spatter spewed from bullet hits.

Thugs twitched and convulsed as the deputies peppered them with bullets.

Felix hit the ground, taking cover.

Ed hesitated, not knowing what to do. His wide eyes flicked about amid the chaos. These guys had paid him to make sure everything went smoothly. This was far from smooth.

27

E d had to choose a side.

He reached for his gun, and the leader of the gang shot him twice before he could draw it. The bullets smacked his chest with a dull thud, and burgundy blood spewed. Ed fell back onto the ground, blood gushing from his thoracic cavity. He struggled for breath on the hot asphalt as spent shell casings danced around him.

The thugs that were still upright took cover behind their cars and the van, continuing to exchange fire with the deputies.

Traffic backed up behind us, and the oncoming traffic had crawled to a stop.

Tango One circled overhead.

Some dude heading south toward Pineapple Bay hopped out of his truck, drew his pistol, and advanced toward the fray.

With the thugs' attention focused on us, they never saw him coming from behind. He darted across the street and took cover behind the lead car in front of the van. He angled his pistol around the vehicle and shot the leader of the gang in the back.

The perp spit up carmine red blood as he fell to the ground. The bullets exited through the front of his chest, spewing a volcano of crimson goo. He flopped to the hot asphalt and twitched for a moment.

It was enough of a distraction to give us the upper hand.

With the thugs' attention split, we were able to take out a few more perps, and less bullets were coming in our direction.

It wasn't long before there was only one thug remaining on his feet besides Felix, who still hugged the roadway.

The final thug dropped his weapon, lifted his arms in the air, and shouted, "Don't shoot!"

The tac team swarmed in, surrounding the perp.

"Face down," I shouted. "On the ground. Now!"

His terrified eyes rounded behind the ski mask, and he complied with my command.

Erickson and Faulkner secured Felix while JD advanced and slapped the cuffs around the last living gang member. JD yanked him to his feet and hauled him back toward the rear of the transport van.

The place looked like a war zone. All of the vehicles were riddled with bullet holes, and a haze of gunpowder still lingered in the air. Spent shell casings peppered the asphalt.

Tango One continued to circle overhead.

Mendoza and Robinson talked to the good Samaritan. He was a former Army guy who just couldn't help lending a hand.

JD frowned as he looked at the damage done to the Porsche. It wasn't long ago when he had the bodywork fixed and the whole thing repainted. The poor car seemed to get trashed all the time.

I put a comforting hand on his shoulder. "Adds character, don't you think?"

Jack scowled at me.

28

The place swarmed with first responders. The medical examiner from Pineapple Bay arrived on the scene and evaluated the bodies. Forensic investigators snapped pictures and documented the scene, making note of every shell casing and bullet hole.

The ringleader of the gang was Felix's son, Javier. He wasn't breathing by the end of the skirmish.

Felix sat in the back of an unmarked patrol car, sobbing. The other thug was put into another vehicle. Deputies from the Pineapple Bay substation arrived on the scene, and red and blue lights flickered. The traffic was at a standstill for miles in both directions.

It didn't take long for news helicopters to arrive, taking aerial footage of the chaos. I fully expected Paris Delaney and her crew to arrive shortly. This was too juicy to pass up, even if it happened just north of Pineapple Bay.

I took the opportunity to speak with Felix.

"I swear, I don't know anything about this," he said. "If I would have known Javier was planning a jailbreak, I would have tried to talk him out of it."

I didn't buy it for one minute. "Bullshit."

"All communications in the jail are monitored. I was not informed of this. There was no mention of it whatsoever. Check the logs."

"Where is Eva Orton?"

"Who?"

"You know who?"

"I don't know who you're talking about," Felix said.

"Javier kidnapped her. What was the plan? Bust you out of prison, escape to Mexico, and use the ransom to live?"

"I don't know anything about a kidnapping. I swear. I'm not saying anything else to you without an attorney."

I frowned at him and closed the door to the unmarked patrol car. I moved to Mendoza's vehicle, opened the back door, and spoke with the surviving thug. "What's your name?"

"I don't have to tell you nothing."

"Doesn't matter. As soon as you get back to the station and we run your prints, we're going to find out who you are. Doesn't make a difference. You're not gonna see daylight for a long time. As in, never."

I ran through the same series of questions with him about Eva Orton.

"I don't know what you're talking about. We didn't kidnap nobody."

"How much money was paid to Ed Collins?"

"Who?"

"You know, the dead transportation officer that gave you the time and the route."

The thug shook his head. "Man, I don't know nothing about nothing."

"I'd start cooperating. You're going down on multiple counts of attempted murder. Play nice, and things might get a little easier for you."

"Fuck you, pig."

"Okay, if that's the way you want to play it."

I slammed the car door in his face and marched back to JD and the others who were standing near the transport van.

One by one, the medical examiner loaded up bodies, and the scene was cleared. Tow trucks hooked up to the perpetrators' vehicles, and a deputy from the Pineapple Bay substation drove the transportation van back to the facility. It was still functional, though it would need some bodywork and a new paint job.

We wrapped up at the scene and headed back to Coconut Key.

JD angled his head around the damage to get a good view out of the windshield. It was webbed with bullet hits. The car looked like hell, but it still drove. Fortunately, the engine was in the rear of the vehicle and suffered no damage. The tires all had air, surprisingly, but the headlights were toast.

People gave us odd looks on the drive home.

JD was in a somber mood. "All that effort, and we didn't get any intel about Eva."

I shrugged. "Maybe they didn't take her."

"I don't know what to think."

At the station, we filled out after-action reports. Afterward, Daniels made good on his word to buy us all beer, even though it hadn't gone as smoothly as he'd hoped.

We went to Flanagan's, and the first round went on the Sheriff's tab. We lifted our glasses to toast—mainly to the fact that we were all still alive.

The news played on the flatscreen behind the bar, showing aerial clips of the shootout over and over again.

From what we could ascertain, Ed Collins acted alone, but it was a shame he didn't survive to be questioned.

Daniels bought a few more rounds, then decided he'd done his duty.

The group dissipated, and we walked a block to Oyster Avenue, looking for trouble. We had no problem finding it.

29

We stopped at *Wetsuit* and grabbed a bite to eat, then ended up at *Tide Pool*. We met Dizzy and Styxx and hung out by the outdoor pool.

"Where's Crash?" I asked.

Styxx shrugged. "I called him, but he didn't answer. He's probably still moping around heartbroken over Faye."

"Understandable."

"He should be glad it's over," Styxx said. "That girl was bad news."

"She was a lot of fun, though," JD muttered.

"You would know," Styxx said.

Dizzy's eyes flicked between the two of them. "Did I miss something?"

"JD had a little rendezvous with Faye before she got together with Crash," Styxx said, his voice thick with disapproval.

Dizzy's eyes rounded. "Man, why am I always the last one to know?"

"You didn't... did you?" JD asked Dizzy.

"No. But now I feel like I missed out."

"The only thing you missed out on is heartache," Styxx said. "She was just a bad influence on Crash all the way around."

"I know Faye could be a little prone to excess, but we all have our indulgences," JD said.

"She OD'd before the show in New York," Styxx exclaimed. "She almost died. And that didn't stop her from using."

I lifted a curious eyebrow. "She was using? What do you mean, like she was still popping pills here and there?"

"You two are detectives. You didn't pick up on it?"

"Pick up on what exactly?" I knew where he was going with this, and I just didn't want to hear it.

"I'm all about partying, but I draw the line at certain things," Styxx said. "I don't put anything up my nose, and I don't stick anything in my veins."

"Tell me Faye wasn't shooting heroin," I said.

Styxx shrugged. "I never saw her jack a vein, but I did see her Chase the Dragon."

Chasing the Dragon was slang for smoking heroin by placing it on a piece of tinfoil, heating it up, then inhaling the vapors through a straw or tube. The wispy shafts of thick smoke that wafted from the tinfoil give the impression of an undulating Dragon, hence the name.

Concern washed over my face.

"See, it's a good thing they broke up," Styxx said.

"Please tell me she didn't get Crash on that shit," I said.

Styxx shrugged.

I groaned. "I know he's been acting a little down in the dumps lately, but I didn't notice anything unusual about his behavior. Have either of you seen any indication he may be using?"

"Not really," Dizzy said.

I pulled my phone from my pocket and dialed Crash's number. It rang a few times then went to voicemail. "Hey, buddy. This is your manager speaking. Just calling to check on you. We are all at Tide Pool. Call me back and let me know you are doing all right."

"I'm thinking maybe we should stop by his apartment just to check on him," JD said.

"I think that's a good idea."

"Want us to go with you?" Dizzy asked.

"No. We're just gonna run over there real quick. I'm sure he's all right," I said.

We walked around the pool, soaking in the delightful visuals that *Tide Pool* had to offer. Waterlogged teeny bikinis were practically bursting at the seams as beauties splashed about. I had a mind to come back and jump in the pool after we checked on Crash.

We walked through the main bar and stepped onto the sidewalk on Oyster Avenue. We had parked the Porsche on a side street.

The tourists were out in full force, and music from live bands spilled into the street. The night was young and full of possibilities. In a few hours, drunken revelers would be listing down the sidewalks like ships tacking against the wind.

We turned the corner onto the side street, and JD clicked the alarm to the Porsche. Only one yellow turn signal flashed. Both the headlights had been shot out, and the bonnet looked like Swiss cheese.

JD stopped in his tracks. "You know I didn't think about how we were going to get home. Probably shouldn't drive without headlights."

It had been daylight when we last left the vehicle.

"Yeah, I would advise against it."

"Deputy Wild," a sultry voice called from behind me.

I turned to see a svelte blonde stalking toward me.

"You following me around?" I asked Sophia.

"It's just a coincidence. Random chance. The Universe has brought us together." She smirked.

I rolled my eyes.

JD drank in her mesmerizing form. "You know, I like you better as a blonde."

She smiled. "Thank you. I don't think Tyson does."

"Whatever gave you that impression?" I asked.

She shrugged. "I had a much easier time seducing you when I was a brunette. I think you have a thing for brunettes."

"I didn't know you were a killer then."

"Should we arrest her," JD asked.

She made a pouty face. "Where's the fun in that?" She paused. "But I could have a good time with you and a pair of handcuffs. I like handcuffs," she said with a naughty sparkle. "You could lock me up and punish me." Her breathy voice was an aphrodisiac. "I need to be punished."

JD swallowed hard.

The air got hotter.

"What are you doing here?"

30

S ophia's eyes rounded, and she grabbed both of our shirts and yanked us to the ground. "Get down!"

As we hit the concrete, gunfire echoed through the night air. Glass shattered, and bullets pelted cars parked on the street. Bullets ricocheted off nearby buildings. The Porsche took a few more hits.

Tires squealed as the perps sped away and rounded the corner onto Oyster Avenue.

Sophia had fallen on top of me. Her heartbeat vibrated my chest, and her plump lips hovered inches away. Her blonde hair dangled in my face.

She smirked. "How many times is that now?"

I didn't answer.

"I think you owe me. I keep saving your ass."

I arched an eyebrow at her.

"Friends of yours?"

"Apparently."

She pushed off me and stood up.

I climbed to my feet and scanned the area.

Curious pedestrians peered around the corner in fear.

The shooters had long since vanished into the night.

"Did you get a good look at the perps?" I asked.

"Silver four-door sedan," Sophia said. "One driver, one passenger—both wearing ski masks. Fully automatic Uzi. Spray and pray."

"You get a plate number?"

"SCG something."

The distant sound of sirens warbled. Someone had called the Sheriff's Department.

"You better get going," I said.

Sophia frowned. "Is that all the thanks I get? I was hoping for a little more." There was a devilish sparkle in her eyes.

She stepped close and took what she wanted. She planted a kiss on my lips.

I didn't kiss back.

She pushed away, spun around, and sauntered toward the corner.

She called over her shoulder, "Stay safe, boys."

We both watched her hips sway as she walked away.

"Are we just going to let a fugitive from justice walk away like that?" JD asked.

"I think so."

"I still don't like her," he said. "But I don't dislike her as much as I did." He paused for a second. "I believe I could put aside my dislike for a brief encounter."

I rolled my eyes.

"What!? I'm just saying. I forgot how captivating she can be."

"That's a good word."

"You said it yourself—she didn't kill Quinn."

"I never said that. I said she claims not to have killed Quinn."

"So, who did?"

I shrugged. "A guy named Holden Cauley, maybe. Who knows?"

Two patrol cars screeched to the scene, lights flashing, painting the nearby buildings a wash of blue and red. The deputies hopped out of their vehicles.

Deputy Takashi shouted. "Wild, Donovan... I should have known you two were involved."

We gave statements to the deputies, and I gave them the partial plate letters and description of the car.

"Any idea who these guys were, or why you were targeted?" Takashi asked.

"Could have something to do with the bust in Pineapple Bay today," I said. "How many Falcon Syndicate members are still out on the street?"

"Maybe that's something you ought to look into," Takashi said.

"I plan on it."

We waited for the forensics team to arrive. They showed up and documented the scene, snapped photos of a few spent shell casings, and collected slugs that were embedded into nearby buildings. With any luck, we might be able to get a ballistics match if the weapons had been used in the commission of another crime.

We wrapped up at the scene, then caught a rideshare to Crash's apartment. We banged on the door several times, but he didn't answer. It was almost 11 PM, and we were starting to get worried.

31

I was about to break down the door when Crash finally pulled it open. His eyes were narrow and bloodshot. He could barely stand. A gust of whiskey from his breath hit me in the face. In an annoyed tone, he growled, "What?!"

He swayed in the doorway.

"We just came by to check on you," I said.

"I'm fine."

"You haven't been answering your phone."

"I gotta pick up my phone every time somebody calls?" he slurred.

"We were just worried about you. You doing alright?"

He forced a smile. "Never better."

"You gonna invite us in?"

"Yeah, sure. Come on in. Join the party." He stepped aside and motioned us in.

We walked into the foyer.

Crash closed the door behind us. "You guys want a drink?"

"No thanks," I said, stepping into the living room. "I think I've had my limit."

"No such thing," Crash slurred.

There was a whiskey bottle on the coffee table that was almost dry. Empty beer bottles were strewn about. The place was a wreck. Dishes piled up in the sink, forming a mountain of roach bait.

"When was the last time you had something to eat?" I asked.

Crash shrugged. "Who needs food?"

"I'm kinda hungry. How about we order a pizza?" I wasn't hungry at all.

"Right on. Pizza party."

"You got any coffee around here?" JD asked.

"I think so. Check the cupboard."

I dialed big Tony's and ordered a pizza for delivery while JD put on a pot of coffee.

Crash flopped onto the couch and reached for the bottle.

"Maybe you ought to slow down."

"Slow down? This is life in the fast lane." He stretched out his arm and made a rock 'n' roll sign.

"Give me the bottle." There were only a few swigs left.

His face crinkled. "Why?"

"Where's your hospitality?"

He looked at me with suspicious eyes but handed the bottle to me.

"Is this about Faye?" I asked.

"Is what about Faye?"

I wiggled the bottle.

"I'm just having a good time."

"Here, all by yourself."

"I just need a little *me time*. It's self-care."

"Looks more like self-destruction."

I glanced around the apartment. I wasn't going to make a big deal out of the bong on the coffee table. I was looking for something a little more illicit. I didn't see anything disturbing right away.

"I know you're going through a tough time."

His red eyes teared up. His face tightened. The waterworks started. Crash sobbed—that drunken, sloppy sob. "She was everything, man."

His chest jerked, and tears streamed down his cheek.

I took a seat next to him on the couch and put my hand on his shoulder. I let him cry it out for a moment.

"I know it's difficult right now, but you've got a great band. You've got great friends and a bright future. Don't piss it all away. We need you."

He sighed and nodded.

"Is there anything I need to be worried about?"

"What do you mean?"

"Are you doing anything else besides drinking?"

He looked at me with caution. "A little herb here and there."

"Anything else?"

"Like what?"

"Like anything that requires a needle?"

His face crinkled. "No way, man. I don't touch that stuff."

I gave him a stern gaze.

He raised his hands innocently. "I swear, man. Don't make a big deal out of this. I just had a few drinks."

"You've had more than a few drinks."

"Am I not allowed to mourn the loss?"

"Just do it in a healthy way. I don't want to go looking for another bass player. You're the best on the island."

Crash lifted his droopy head. Then a slight smirk tugged his lips. "I'm the best on the planet."

I laughed. "Maybe."

The coffee pot percolated, and the aroma filled the apartment. JD poured a cup, mixed in cream and sugar, and delivered it to Crash.

He let it cool a moment before sipping the coffee. "Can we put a little whiskey in this?"

I shook my head.

"Party pooper."

It wasn't long before the delivery guy banged on the door. I climbed off the couch and ambled down the foyer. I paid the guy in cash, and he handed me the cardboard box of steaming pizza. I brought it back into the living room and set it on the coffee table after pushing aside the empty beer bottles. I lifted the lid, and steam wafted from the gooey pizza, covered in toppings.

Crash pulled off a slice, and the stringy cheese stretched about a foot before it snapped.

We all chowed down, and Crash ended up devouring over half of the pizza. He probably hadn't eaten all day.

We hung out at the apartment for a while as Crash became more lucid. I listened to him moan about Faye for the next hour. With a full belly and having vented, he passed out on the couch, despite the cup of coffee. His respiration was good, so I wasn't too concerned.

JD and I cleaned up the apartment, poured out the rest of the whiskey, and took the remaining few beer bottles from the fridge. It was after 1 AM when we helped Crash off the couch and escorted him to the bedroom. He flopped on top of the covers and passed out fully dressed.

I didn't want Crash to meet the typical rock star demise, so I told JD I'd sleep on the couch and keep a watch on him during the night.

"How are we going to handle this?" JD asked.

"I think he's just blowing off a little steam."

"Let's hope that's all this is."

Jack left, and I rummaged through the apartment, looking for a spare blanket. I turned the couch into a makeshift bed and tried to get comfortable. It didn't have a lot of support. Needless to say, I didn't get a good night's sleep.

I got up a few times to check on Crash, and he seemed to be doing okay. I slipped out before sunrise and caught a rideshare back to the marina. Buddy was excited to see me. I leashed him up, took him out for a walk, then decided to crawl in bed for a few more hours.

I climbed up to my stateroom, and there was an interesting surprise waiting for me.

32

I had to ask myself, was it me? Was I inviting this kind of drama into my life? I was like catnip for crazies and psychos.

Sophia Breslin was curled up in my bed.

She yawned and stretched and peeled an eye open. She rolled to face me, and the covers slipped away, revealing a round, perky breast. "You missed out last night. Where were you? Having fun with some floozy?"

I laughed. "Babysitting a drunken bandmate."

She made an adorable face. "Aw, you're so caring. I think that's what I like about you. You're ruthless, but you're a sweetheart underneath it all."

"What are you doing here?"

She lifted a sassy eyebrow. "What do you think I'm doing here? I was looking for a good time."

She pulled away the rest of the covers, revealing her naked form. Her graceful curves were inspiring. "See what you missed out on."

I couldn't help but soak in her beauty.

"It's not too late. I'm a fan of morning sex, how about you?"

I was a fan of it whenever I could get it—day or night didn't matter. But she was out of her mind if she thought I was gonna hop in the sack with her.

I'm not gonna lie, I gave it serious consideration for a minute... or two. Maybe three.

"I don't have any weapons. You can frisk me if you'd like," she said with a diabolical grin.

"Oh, you have weapons, alright."

"My charm *is* deadly." Her eyes smoldered. "You can handcuff me if it will make you feel safer."

Tempting.

"I know you get a lot of ass, Tyson. But are you really going to turn this down?"

She knew exactly what she had to offer.

The devil on my shoulder whispered—screamed—in my ear. Maybe she didn't kill Quinn Palmer. Maybe I'd been too harsh in my judgment. The little brain teamed up with the devil and added to the discussion. Even my voice of reason was making compelling arguments. Her tight, toned midriff, her round, supple orbs and perky peaks. Her plump assets. Her smooth legs. Her pillowy soft lips. Her mesmerizing eyes. Her breathy voice that loved to moan the naughtiest of phrases. Her eagerness to please. The danger and excitement of it all.

With every passing second, my willpower weakened. My cognitive function declined as blood flow rushed south. I began to roast in the flames of desire.

33

I was on the verge of a bad decision when Sheriff Daniels called and spoiled the mood.

"I need you and numbnuts to get down to the station ASAP."

"What's going on?"

"Two divers found something I think you're gonna want to have a look at."

I groaned. "I'll be right there."

I ended the call and slipped the phone back into my pocket. I frowned and exhaled a deep breath. "Sorry. Duty calls."

"Your loss."

"You showed yourself in. You can show yourself out."

"Have a nice day, dear," she mocked.

I rolled my eyes, marched out of the stateroom, and plummeted down the steps to the main deck. I grabbed my helmet and gloves and jogged to the dock. I called JD along the way and gave him an update.

I hopped on the bike and zipped across town to the Sheriff's Department. JD pulled into the parking lot a moment later with the stereo blasting. He had called a mobile windshield replacement company to come to his house and fix the demolished glass after hours. Jack had a connection for everything. Visibility was good now, but the headlights were still a mess. He looked bright and cheery. I'm glad he got a full night's sleep. Meanwhile, I was stiff and sore from the couch and sleep-deprived, not to mention worked up.

Daniels greeted us on the dock with a dive team and the medical examiner. We trotted to the patrol boat and climbed aboard.

I cast off the lines, and Daniels cranked up the engines and idled us out of the marina. He brought the boat on plane, and the engines growled. The Defender class aluminum patrol boat carved through the swells, and the teal water glistened with the morning sun. The outboards spit a frothy wake as the boat bounced across the water, spraying mists of saltwater.

"Want to give me more details?" I shouted over the rumble of the engines.

"Two recreational divers found a steamer trunk at the bottom of the ocean north of Barracuda Key. When they popped it open, they found the body inside."

I cringed. "Eva Orton?"

"That's my guess."

"How did they find it?"

"Amateur treasure hunters. I guess they were out fiddle-farting around with sonar and discovered the object. They made a quick dive and discovered the body."

JD gave me a worried look. I knew what he was concerned about. We had discovered the wreckage of an old French ship not long ago—40 brass cannons and a handful of gold coins. We were pretty sure we'd found the lost treasure of Jaques De La Fontaine, the infamous French pirate. We hadn't been to the dive site in a while, but we were confident that nobody else knew where it was. It had been down there for over 400 years, and we happened to stumble across it. We had started the search in a few areas north of Barracuda Key, and rumors circulated about treasure in the area. Fortunately, our dive site was far removed from Barracuda Key.

Year after year, the island drew treasure hunters with dollar signs in their eyes. As technology advanced, it was only a matter of time before every sunken ship was discovered.

JD muttered in my ear, "We need to get back to work on Operation Salvage. I'm thinking we need to do that sooner rather than later."

It didn't take too long to reach the divers. They were in a 35-foot sport-yacht with navy blue trim. We pulled alongside their boat and spoke briefly.

"We left her down there," Chuck, one of the divers, said. "We didn't want to disturb anything or contaminate evidence."

By this point in time, there wouldn't be much usable evidence. There was no telling how long Eva had been buried underwater in the trunk.

Chuck and his buddy, Mark, gave us a full statement. They had boated down from Fort Lauderdale and were planning on spending a week in the Keys, diving reefs and shipwrecks and looking for treasure.

JD had inquired about the type of sonar drone they were using. I knew him well—he was assessing their threat level. After interrogating them, he muttered to me, "The drone they are using is junk. They're never going to find anything."

"Looks like they found something," I said dryly.

After talking to Mark and Chuck, it was clear they had nothing to do with Eva's disappearance and had only gotten into town yesterday. I made a few phone calls, and their wives verified their stories.

The county dive team plunged into the water. It didn't take them long to recover Eva's remains. Bubbles roiled the surface, and the divers brought up her pale corpse. The remains were transferred to the patrol boat.

Eva's body lay on the deck, her milky eyes staring at the sky, her blonde hair twisted and ratted. Her skin was ghostly, and her lips almost blue. She looked like a vampire, minus the fangs.

I studied the body carefully. It was Eva Orton alright. There was no doubt about it.

"How long has she been down there?" Daniels asked.

"Hard to say," Brenda replied, hovering over the remains, wearing pink nitrile gloves. "A few days at least. I'll know more when I get her back to the lab."

"So, she could have been killed the day of her abduction," I said.

Brenda nodded.

"That would explain why the kidnappers didn't give proof of life," JD said.

"Maybe she became unruly and put up a struggle," I suggested.

"Somebody kidnaps me, I'm certainly going to become unruly," JD said.

"You already are unruly," Daniels muttered.

"Nolan's not gonna like this," I said.

34

Bubbles from the divers surfaced, and their blurry shapes squiggled under the water as they ascended. They broke through the water an instant later, four of them clinging onto a large brown steamer trunk, finished with fine leather. It had latches, straps, and brass rivets. Handles on either side of the trunk allowed better grip.

This was no cheap item. I'd seen some of these vintage trunks go for up to $15,000.

The divers had turned it upside down and used the regulators to fill it with air, allowing it to float to the surface more easily.

We hoisted the heavy thing onto the boat and examined it. The inside of the trunk was empty. The leather lining had slight bloodstains that had mostly been washed away by the saltwater. It was my guess that Eva sat in the trunk for a while before being submerged.

The blood indicated trauma and coincided with Brenda's finding of a gash on the back of her scalp—an indication of blunt force trauma. She had a cracked skull.

"The killer stuffed her into a steamer trunk and dumped her in the ocean," JD said.

"It would appear that way," Daniels said.

"That's a pretty pricey trunk to toss in the water," JD added.

"Maybe that's all they had," I said.

"I don't know about you, but I'd have found a cheap trunk. Just saying."

Jack had a point.

We cut Chuck and Mark loose and headed back toward Coconut Key. I called Nolan along the way and informed him of the bad news. It didn't come as a shock, and he handled it better than I anticipated. I kept the details limited for the time being. "Your wife didn't happen to own a steamer trunk did she?"

"No. I don't believe so. Why do you ask?"

"This is unpleasant, but we found the remains crammed into the trunk at the bottom of the ocean."

"Good God. That's barbaric."

"I'll send you a picture of the trunk. Tell me if you recognize it."

I snapped a photo and texted it to him. A moment later, Nolan said. "No. I've never seen that before."

"You're sure?"

"Eva had a healthy spending habit. She could have purchased that without my knowledge, but I don't recall seeing it around the house."

"We need you to come down to the morgue to make a positive ID."

"When do you need me to do that?"

"I'll have the medical examiner's office call you."

He was silent for a long moment. "Thank you for pursuing this case to a conclusion."

"Again, I'm sorry for your loss. It's not the outcome I had hoped for."

"Any luck tracking down the kidnappers' crypto wallet?"

"No," I said.

"So, I paid $100 million for nothing? And the scumbags are going to get away with it."

"I wish I could say that what comes around goes around, but in my experience, sometimes bad people get away with bad things. But I assure you, we're not giving up on this case. The investigation is only beginning."

35

P aris Delaney and her news crew waited for us on the dock at the station. They filmed as we transferred Eva's remains onto a gurney. She was wheeled down the dock to the medical examiner's van, and the body bag was loaded inside.

We unloaded the trunk and set it on the dock, dripping wet. The news crew continued to film as we let it drip dry.

As usual, Paris approached and asked a barrage of questions, the camera lens zooming in on me. "Can you identify the victim?"

"We discovered the remains of Eva Orton between here and Barracuda Key. If anyone has information or has seen anything suspicious, please contact the Sheriff's Department immediately."

"So this will be proceeding as a homicide investigation?"

"Yes, it will."

"What can you tell us about the steamer trunk?"

"It was used to dispose of the remains. Again, if anyone has seen this trunk or can identify any suspects, please contact the department."

I answered a few more questions. I was happy to get the information out to the public on the off chance that somebody had seen something.

We hauled the steamer trunk down the dock and logged it into evidence. Afterward, we filled out after-action reports in the conference room, typing away on iPads under the pale green fluorescent lighting.

By the time we were done, my stomach was rumbling. I'd skipped breakfast and was feeling thin from lack of sleep.

I hopped on my bike, and JD followed me back to *Diver Down*. We took a seat at the bar, and Teagan greeted us with a sad face. "I saw the news that you found Eva's remains."

I gave her a somber nod.

"I just had this funny vibe that she was in a confined space." She shivered. "I can't imagine." Teagan paused, and her face crinkled. "This is going to sound terrible, but I hope she wasn't still alive when she was stuffed in that steamer trunk and thrown in the water."

"I think the blunt force trauma to the head did her in first."

"What a horrible way to go." She shivered again. "Oh, I want to tell you... I saw this blonde woman walking Buddy. I figured she was one of your *friends*," Teagan said in air quotes, trying not to sound jealous. "But I just wanted to make sure she wasn't trying to abduct him or anything."

I chuckled. "I know the blonde. I don't know if I would cate-gorize her as a *friend*."

Teagan gave me a look.

I raised my hands innocently. "I swear, I've had no involve-ment with that woman... Recently," I muttered.

She rolled her eyes and changed the subject. "Are you guys hungry?"

We both nodded.

Jack ordered the Chilean sea bass with jumbo lump crab au gratin and sautéed spinach. I ordered the blackened salmon with shrimp, scallops, and crawfish in a white wine cream sauce with dirty rice.

Needless to say, the meal was tasty.

Daniels called as we finished up. "Brenda's just getting started, but she found fluid in Eva's lungs. She was still alive when she was dumped overboard."

I winced.

"Damn savages," Daniels muttered.

"What's wrong with people?"

"When you figure that out, let me know. In the meantime, get over to Sandpiper Point. There's a dockhand that recog-nized the steamer trunk. Saw it on the news. Says he remembers seeing a guy wheel it down the dock on a dolly and load it aboard a boat. Said he didn't think much of it at the time, but it struck him as odd."

"Does he know the guy? Does he remember the name of the boat?"

"He's not sure. Doesn't remember the name of the boat either. Says he was busy doing other things at the time and had forgotten all about it until he saw Paris's report. Maybe she's not so bad after all."

"What's the dock hand's name?"

"Derek Bartley."

"We're on it," I said.

We finished up, then took the Porsche over to Sandpiper Point. The car was battered and bruised, but still drivable. It was an upscale marina filled with luxury yachts, sport boats, and nice sailboats. It was on the pricier end of the spectrum and was home to tech gurus, doctors, young lawyers, and a few celebrities.

We inquired in the office about Derek and were told where we could find him.

Derek was a young guy in his early 20s with dark hair and a muscular build. He was about 6'1" and wore a royal blue polo shirt with a Sandpiper Point logo embroidered on the chest. He wore white cargo shorts and deck shoes.

Derek had a myriad of duties around the marina. Everything from maintaining the grounds to restroom sanitation. He helped customers at the fuel dock, helped with cargo and tying up and casting off lines. He assisted with storage units, boat rentals, and just about anything else the tenants might need.

We found him on the dock helping a tenant castoff. We flashed our badges and made introductions.

"Can you describe the guy you saw with the steamer trunk?" I asked.

"Yeah, he was a stocky guy. Bald. Maybe 5'10", mid-30s."

I exchanged a glance with JD.

"And you're sure the trunk he had was the same one you saw on TV?"

Derek nodded. "Pretty sure. I mean, I was busy at the time. It gets really hectic around here. I just remember seeing him wheel the trunk down the dock and thinking it was kinda cool, actually. My girlfriend's been wanting one, but those damn things are expensive. I'm talking *used-car* expensive."

I pulled up a picture of Jason Bradley on my phone and showed it to Derek.

"Is that the guy?"

"Yeah, that's him."

A slight smirk tugged my lips, and I exchanged another glance with JD. We were getting closer.

I asked Derek to come down to the station to make a sworn affidavit. He did, and we were able to get an arrest warrant for Jason Bradley and a warrant to search Nolan's residence.

We rounded up a tactical team, which consisted of the usual suspects—Faulkner, Erickson, Mendoza, and Robinson. We left the station and headed over to the posh neighborhood of Stingray Bay.

36

We pulled up to Nolan's house and parked across the street. The two silver SUVs still occupied the curb in front of the house. I rang the bell at the gate to the courtyard. No need to go in with guns blazing. Not yet, anyway.

Nolan's voice crackled through the speaker a moment later. "Deputy Wild, I was just about to leave for the morgue. How can I help you?"

"We have a few additional questions for Jason."

"He's not here at the moment."

"Do you know where he is?"

"No, I don't. He left not too long ago. Is there some kind of problem?"

"We have a warrant for his arrest and a warrant to search the premises."

Nolan stammered, "You don't think he's got something to do with Eva's death, do you?"

"Yes, we do. I have a witness that places him at Sandpiper Point with the trunk that Eva was found in."

Nolan gasped. "Are you sure? Eyewitness testimony is notoriously inaccurate."

"That's why we'd like to bring him in for further questioning. You want to buzz us inside, or do I have to break down this gate?"

"Yes, of course."

The gate buzzed, and we pushed into the courtyard and rushed to the front door.

Nolan opened a moment later, and his eyes rounded at the sight of deputies with tactical gear and assault rifles. He stepped aside as we flooded into the home. The deputies fanned out, searching the vast estate. We stayed behind in the foyer and spoke with Nolan for a moment.

I regarded him with a healthy dose of suspicion.

I showed him a picture of the steamer trunk again. "Are you sure you've never seen this before?"

He looked frazzled as he studied the image for a moment. "Maybe. Eva had so many clothes and shoes. Her closet is bigger than my first apartment. It's possible that the trunk was here in the house, perhaps in her closet, and I didn't notice it."

It was a convenient backtrack.

"And you're sure you don't know where Jason is at the moment?"

"No, I don't know where he is, Deputy. I don't particularly like your implication. If Jason is responsible somehow, I will do everything in my power to assist you. I want my wife's killer or killers brought to justice. But I'm having a hard time believing Jason was involved. I vet my employees thoroughly."

"And yet one of them was having an affair with your wife, and another may have murdered her."

His eyes narrowed at me.

"Does Jason have a girlfriend? What about friends or associates?"

"I stay out of the private lives of my employees."

"If only they would have stayed out of yours."

I called Isabella and asked her to track Jason's phone. With a few keystrokes, she was able to tell me it was off the grid. Jason had probably seen the news and figured he would be picked up at any moment.

He was officially *on the run.*

Before ending the call, Isabella said, "By the way, that name you gave me... Holden Cauley... He's a contract hitter."

"And?"

"No recent activity as far as I can tell. Not since Quinn's death. But that doesn't mean anything. He could have gone dark or retired."

"Or he could be dead."

"Do not fall for her BS, Tyson."

"I won't."

I called Sheriff Daniels and told him the suspect wasn't here. He said he'd send deputies to Jason's apartment. I asked the sheriff to set up checkpoints on the highway at the north side of the island and to contact airport security. The TSA could pick Jason up if he tried to leave the country through the commercial terminal.

The FBO was a different story.

You could walk through the terminal to the tarmac, and nobody would say a word. Private flights weren't bound by the same security regulations.

"I'll send a deputy out to the FBO just in case he turns up," Daniels said. "I'll notify the Coast Guard and send somebody over to Sandpiper Point in case he tries to get out of here on his boat. According to the registration records, he's got a 32-foot sport yacht named *Bruiser*. He's not getting away," Daniels assured.

W e'd been through Nolan's house before, looking for any signs of an abduction. This time, I was looking for signs of murder. I played out different scenarios in my head, trying to come up with a motive.

Why would Jason kill Eva?

Were they having an affair?

Did they get into a fight?

Or had Jason killed her at Nolan's request?

It was cheaper than a divorce. But only if you didn't get caught.

We searched the guest bedrooms and bathrooms, along with the master bedroom. It was a sprawling space with a four-post canopy bed and *his and hers* closets that were indeed larger than most apartments.

Eva's closet was filled with designer gowns in a variety of cuts and colors. She could have worn a new dress every day of the week for the next several years and never have worn the same thing twice. There were rows and rows of shoes— spike heeled Manolo Blahnik's, flats, strappy suede heels with open toes... Every imaginable style and color, most with little or no wear on the soles.

There were oodles of coats, blouses, and skirts. Three full-length mirrors made the closet look like a department store fitting room, offering multiple angles of views. There was no need to ask anyone how your backside looked—you could see for yourself.

A dresser in the center of the closet had drawers for unmentionables, T-shirts, and jeans. There was a display case for high-end jewelry. Diamond necklaces sparkled, rings glittered, earrings dangled from golden trees. It was like walking into a designer boutique. Many of the clothing articles were bespoke, tailor-made to Eva's measurements.

There were bleached hardwoods in the master bedroom and closets. The bathroom was tiled with luxurious Italian marble. There was a large Jacuzzi tub, a futuristic toilet, and a bidet. There were *his and hers* sinks and a grooming station with a magnifying mirror attached to the wall on an articulated arm. The walk-in shower stall had a glass door and a removable showerhead.

The accommodations were the epitome of style and luxury.

With blunt force trauma to the head, Eva would've bled considerably. The forensic investigators sprayed Luminol, a chemiluminescent substance that would glow when mixed with an oxidizing agent like iron in hemoglobin. Unfortunately, it also reacted to other oxidizing agents such as copper, bleach, horseradish, urine, fecal material, and smoke residue.

It only glows for about 30 seconds, and the room needs to be dimmed. Forensic investigators would typically snap extended exposure photos to capture the reaction. The team moved through the house room by room, looking for any signs of trauma.

Unfortunately, the bathrooms and basins had all been scrubbed with bleach, causing the surfaces to react with the Luminol, concealing any blood spatter that may have been present.

Maybe Eva was attacked in the house. Maybe she wasn't.

Nolan watched with concerned eyes, pacing around nervously. I couldn't tell if his distress came from the fact he'd hired a guy like Jason or if he had some involvement in Eva's death. So far, he remained cooperative, and we had no reason to arrest him.

We wrapped up, and I told Nolan to contact me if he heard from Jason. "Oh, and don't leave town," I said as I stepped onto the front porch.

His face tensed. "I had no involvement in Eva's death, I can assure you."

"Did I mention she was still alive when the trunk was tossed overboard?"

Nolan's eyes rounded, and his jaw dropped. "What!?" The color drained from his face and his eyes misted. "That's horrible."

His hands trembled, and tears streamed down his cheek.

"I need to sit down," he said, unsteady. "If you'll excuse me."

He closed the door, and I felt bad for laying it on him like that. I wanted to get a reaction, and I did. I couldn't quite tell if that was guilt or sorrow.

I needed a vacation. I was starting to get jaded. Everyone looked like a crook.

38

There was a BOLO out for Jason Bradley. Deputies staked out *Sandpiper Point*. His boat was still there. Between the checkpoints on the island and the Coast Guard, I hoped we'd pick him up before he managed to flee the area. There was no doubt in my mind he would try to get as far away from Coconut Key as possible.

I sure as hell would.

I called several members of Nolan's security staff. Most of them claimed not to know much about Jason's personal life, but Will told me, "I think his girlfriend's name is Victoria. I met her once."

"Do you know her last name?"

He thought for a moment. "Ross, I think. She lives in the Sirona Springs apartments. I was with Jason when he dropped something off at her place once."

I thanked him for the info.

"You think he really killed Eva?"

"He's high on the list."

"Between you and me," Will muttered. "I never really liked that guy. Guess Nolan will be looking for a new head of security."

"Maybe you'll be next in line," I said.

Will chuckled. "Maybe."

I ended the call and dialed Denise. After a brief search, she gave me the address and apartment number for Victoria Ross. JD and I headed over to the Sirona Springs.

It was a nice two-story complex with parking underneath. The colonial-style building was painted white with forest green shutters. French doors opened onto small balconies. Two blocks from the beach, it wasn't a bad location.

We parked at the curb, climbed the steps, and pushed into the lobby. We took the stairs up to the second floor and ambled down the hall to find apartment #204. I knocked on the door and waited for a reply.

I heard movement inside, and a moment later, a woman's voice shouted through the door. "Who is it?"

"Coconut County," I said, holding my badge to the peephole. "We need to speak with you regarding Jason Bradley."

She pulled open the door and looked at us with cautious eyes. "What's going on?"

Victoria was an attractive woman. She had short auburn hair that dangled above her shoulders. With steel blue eyes, burgundy lips, and tan skin, she wasn't bad to look at. She was early 30s and had a nice figure. Maybe just a little out of Jason's league. Maybe a lot.

"Is he here, ma'am?"

She shook her head.

"Have you seen him at all today?"

"No, why?"

"Has he been in contact with you?"

She shook her head again. "I don't understand. Is there some kind of problem?"

"We have a warrant for his arrest."

Her eyes rounded, and she swallowed hard.

"You mind if we take a look around your apartment?"

She hesitated a moment and squirmed. "He's not here. I can assure you of that. What is he accused of?"

"He's wanted in connection with the kidnapping and murder of Eva Orton."

She gasped, and her worried eyes rounded. She processed the information, then shook her head. "No. Jason is not capable of something like that."

"If that's the case, then he's got nothing to worry about. As it stands, he's a fugitive, and he has a lot of explaining to do."

She stared at us for a moment, paralyzed with fear and concern.

"I'll ask again, do you mind if we look around?"

"Sure," she stammered. "I've got nothing to hide."

She stepped aside and motioned us into the apartment. We entered and marched down the foyer to the living room.

The apartment was quaint and cozy. The walls were pastel yellow, and there were lots of plants that got plenty of sunlight and water.

We gave a quick glance around, searching the master bedroom, the closets, and the guest bath. Then we returned to the living room.

"Satisfied?"

I nodded.

"I told you he wasn't here."

"How long have you been seeing each other?" I asked.

"A little over a year."

I noticed an engagement ring on her finger. "Is it serious?"

She held up her hand, wiggling her fingers. The elegant diamond sparkled. It wasn't enormous, but respectable.

"When's the date?"

"I don't see how that's any of your business."

I dug in my pocket and gave her my card. "If you see or hear from Jason, please contact me immediately. I'm sure I don't need to remind you that assisting a fugitive is a criminal act."

"You're making a mistake. Jason didn't have anything to do with Eva Orton's death."

She folded her arms and glared at us.

"Thanks for your cooperation, ma'am," I said before spinning around and marching toward the door.

She closed and latched it behind us after we exited.

"Think she's heard from him?" JD asked as we walked down the hallway.

"We're about to find out." I pulled my phone from my pocket and called Isabella. I asked her to give me the call logs for Victoria's phone and monitor the incoming calls.

Isabella worked her magic. A moment later, she said, "Victoria got a call from a prepaid cellular about 20 minutes ago. The call originated from a self-storage facility on the east side of the island."

"Where's the phone now?"

"Off the grid," Isabella said. "I'll let you know if it pops up."

"Thanks," I said before ending the call.

I dialed Sheriff Daniels and had him send a patrol unit to the storage facility. But I figured Jason would be long gone.

JD and I left the apartment building and walked down the block to the Porsche. The street ran perpendicular to the beach and ended with a sandy outlet. The waves crashed against the teal shore. Pedestrians strolled the block, and beachgoers came and went. The squawk of gulls drifted with the breeze. The palm trees that lined the avenue swayed overhead.

We climbed into the car and watched the main entrance to Victoria's building. A few pedestrians strolled the sidewalk. A cute girl passed on a mountain bike. A tabby cat stalked its prey in the shrubs of the apartment complex.

30 minutes had passed when Isabella called again. "Victoria just got another incoming call from the burner phone."

"Where was it at?"

"On the move. Looks like the phone was traveling in a car heading east on Hemmingway, then turned north onto Puffer Park. After the call ended, the burner dropped from the network. He must have switched it off."

"Something's up," I said.

"I'll let you know if the device pops up again."

I called Daniels and gave him an update. "Send a few patrol units to that area and see if they can spot Jason's vehicle."

"A black four-door Lexus is registered in his name, but he could be in a cab," Daniels said. "You'd have to be pretty stupid to drive around in your own vehicle with every deputy in the department looking for you."

"Could be in a stolen vehicle."

"Hopefully, we'll get lucky," Daniels said before hanging up.

We sat parked at the curb. After a few minutes, Victoria stepped out of her apartment building and plunged down the steps. A small black duffel bag dangled from her shoulder as she scampered to the street.

A silver compact car pulled to the curb. Victoria hopped into the back, and the car sped away.

JD cranked up the engine, and the rideshare drove right past us. Victoria was too preoccupied to notice.

JD banked a u-turn and followed after them.

The rideshare turned left at the beach and headed north on Casa Vista, then took another left on Dumont.

We caught up to them pretty quickly but kept a safe distance. I watched Victoria in the backseat. Her head was down as she fumbled for something in her purse.

"Where do you think she's headed?" JD asked.

"To meet up with Jason."

"One last rendezvous before he slips town?"

"Maybe she's going with him."

The rideshare took a right on Seaview Lane, heading north. It didn't take long to figure out exactly where she was going.

39

It came as no surprise that Victoria was headed to the FBO at the Coconut Key airport. The rideshare pulled to the drop-off point, and Victoria hopped out of the vehicle and rushed into the terminal.

The silver car sped away, and JD zipped the Porsche around to take its place.

I hopped out and marched into the terminal as Victoria hustled through to the tarmac. A *Slipstream G650* waited for her, along with a man in a gray suit. He had shaggy brown hair and dark sunglasses. He waved at her, standing at the base of the steps to the aircraft next to the pilot.

Victoria trotted to greet him.

I did a double-take.

It was Jason wearing a bad wig. I broke into a sprint, running onto the tarmac.

Jason saw me and drew a pistol from his shoulder holster. He put the black semiautomatic to the pilot's head and moved behind him for cover. He shouted, "Back off!"

I held up and drew my weapon.

Jason backed up the steps to the aircraft, dragging the pilot along.

The pilot's eyes were bathed in fear, and his face misted with sweat. He cooperated with Jason, and the two fumbled their way into the sleek aircraft.

It was too risky for me to take a shot.

The pilot retracted the steps and closed the door to the fuselage.

I grumbled under my breath, holstered my pistol, and called Sheriff Daniels.

"Get in touch with air traffic control. Tell them we've got a hostage situation." I gave him the tail number of the aircraft. "Tell them not to clear that aircraft for takeoff."

By this time, JD had parked the car and jogged to meet me on the tarmac.

This was about to get ugly.

Sirens warbled in the distance, drawing closer. Pretty soon, the area would be swarming with Feds, Homeland Security, airport security, and any other agency that had an interest.

The Slipstream started taxing toward the runway. Air traffic control would have to alert the other planes and put incoming flights in a holding pattern, or things could get messy.

I tried calling the burner phone Jason used to call Victoria. To my surprise, he answered. "Who is this?"

"It's Deputy Wild. You're about to have a real bad day if you keep on your present course of action."

"How did you get this number?"

"Let's not waste time with things that don't really matter. What matters is that you turn this ship around before anybody else gets hurt."

"You tell air traffic control to clear the runways, or I'm going to start putting holes in people."

"Do you know how to fly the plane?"

Jason said nothing.

"You're going to run out of people to put holes in. How many are on board? The pilot, a flight attendant, maybe two? Are you going to put holes into your girlfriend?"

"Clear the runway, or there's going to be blood on your hands." There was a slight quiver in his voice.

The plane kept rolling toward the runway.

Another pilot maneuvered his plane to block Jason's path.

"I think you bit off more than you can chew," I said. "How do you see this working out?"

"I see it working out just fine once I get off the ground. Get that fucking plane out of my way."

"Where will you go? There will be an international warrant for your arrest. You can't run from this."

"Yes, I can. There are still places beyond your reach."

"Beyond my reach?"

"If you think I'm going to hint at where I'm going, you're sadly mistaken. Don't try to negotiate with me, Deputy Wild. It's not going to work."

"How much fuel do you have?"

"Enough."

"What about Victoria?"

"What about her?"

"Is this the life she really wants? To be a fugitive? Never able to return to the United States? Let me tell you, being on the run gets old after a while."

"Spending the rest of your life in a jail cell gets old," Jason replied.

"Why did you do it? Why did you kill Eva?"

"I didn't kill anyone."

"Then why are you running?"

He said nothing.

"You dumped her in the ocean in a steamer trunk while she was still alive."

He remained silent.

"Didn't know she was alive, did you?"

There was another long pause.

"Get that plane out of my way, or people start dying."

40

A baggage cart blocked one side of the plane, and a fire truck blocked another. The plane was quickly surrounded by emergency vehicles, which only agitated Jason.

"Move these vehicles out of my way, and clear the runway for takeoff!" Jason demanded. His snarling voice crackled through the speaker in my phone.

He barked commands to me and to the pilot, who relayed them to the tower.

"Have you thought about what happens when you get in the air?" I asked.

"Yeah, I've thought about it. It means I will be free."

"Not exactly. Once you're airborne, if you even get off the ground, you'll become a national security threat. They take that kind of thing seriously after 9/11. The Feds will be here any minute. The FAA is coordinating with the military. This thing is about to get out of hand. It will not end well for you.

You and your girlfriend are looking at federal time. I know you don't want that for her. Open the door, let the hostages out, and surrender. I'll make sure you get a fair shake."

Unmarked cars and black SUVs screeched onto the tarmac. The Feds had arrived. Men in suits hopped out and made their way toward me. A black military-style transport rumbled onto the scene, and federal agents decked out with tactical gear, helmets, and AR-15s flooded out and took position.

I had no doubt snipers would soon be perched on rooftops.

Tango One pattered overhead, having been given clearance into the restricted airspace of the airport. There was a black helicopter that I'm sure belonged to a 3-letter agency. A gray UH-1Y Venom gunship arrived, complete with Hydra 70 air-to-ground rockets and .50 machine guns. I was pretty sure it came from the Naval Air Station.

"Last chance," I said to Jason. "The Feds are about to take the lead on this. How about you let one of the hostages go as a sign of good faith?"

I displayed my badge to the FBI guys as they stepped to me.

"Special Agent Sam Ferguson," one of them said, displaying his credentials. "This is my partner Special Agent Chris Greenway. Are you in contact with the hijacker?"

I nodded.

"Not to step on your toes, but this is a federal matter, and we'll be taking the lead."

I handed him my cell phone and gave him a brief rundown of the situation.

Sam introduced himself to Jason.

I heard Jason's voice crackle back through the speaker. "What happened to Tyson? I want to talk to Tyson?"

"You're dealing with me now," Sam said.

"Put Tyson back on the phone, or somebody dies?"

"Can't do that."

"I'm not fucking around."

"Sounds like you're upset," Sam said in a slow, smooth voice.

"You're goddamn right, I'm upset. Get these vehicles out of my way and clear the runway for takeoff."

"I can't do that. But what I can do is help you out. I know you think I'm the bad guy. But I'm just here to ensure the best possible outcome for everyone."

"The best possible outcome for everyone?" Jason scoffed. "That outcome involves me in custody. And that's not going to happen."

Commotion filtered through the speaker. There was a scream, followed by a loud bang. Agent Ferguson pulled the device away from his ear momentarily.

"Jason? What's happening?"

There was no response.

Sam repeated the question.

"I'll tell you what's happening," Jason shouted into the phone.

A moment later, the door to the aircraft unlatched, and Jason swung it open and pushed the body of a flight attendant out. The lifeless corpse tumbled to the tarmac and splattered crimson blood, her limbs flopping at unnatural angles. A pool of blood oozed from the body.

My heart sank, and my jaw tightened.

"That's what's happening," Jason growled in the doorway.

41

B efore Jason could close the door to the fuselage, an FBI sniper took a shot.

The rifle's report echoed across the tarmac, rippling through the air. The bullet smacked Jason in the chest, tumbling him back into the fuselage. Blood splattered, and shrieks of terror spilled out of the plane and through the speaker in my phone.

Agent Sam Ferguson sighed and handed the phone back to me without looking.

I took it from him, ended the call, and slipped the phone into my pocket.

Emergency responders rushed toward the aircraft.

The passengers were deplaned, and EMTs and paramedics evaluated them for injuries.

Jason was dead before he hit the ground.

Victoria was taken into custody. She sobbed and wailed, her face contorted with loss. She was stuffed into the back of a patrol car and taken to the station for processing.

Brenda was called to the scene to examine the remains of the victim and the hijacker. Their bodies were loaded into bags and transferred to the medical examiner's van.

Red and blue lights flickered, and first responders hustled about. The entire airport was shut down for several hours.

It wasn't exactly the resolution I had hoped for, and it left me with many unanswered questions.

We filled out after-action reports at the station and finally got around to interviewing Victoria. She had been placed into an interrogation room and had spent a few hours there by the time we got to her.

Her eyes were red and puffy from crying. She trembled with nerves, and the color had drained from her face. The pale green glow of the overhead fluorescent lights didn't do much to improve her sickly pallor.

JD and I took a seat across the table from her.

"Did Jason say anything to you about Eva's murder?"

She shook her head.

"Right now, you're looking at serious charges—aiding and abetting a fugitive, kidnapping, conspiracy, and a host of other goodies."

Her terrified eyes rounded even further. "I didn't do anything."

"You attempted to hijack a plane and flee the country with your boyfriend, a known fugitive. I would say that's doing *something*."

"I didn't know he was going to do that. All he told me was that I needed to meet him at the airport, and we needed to get out of town. I asked him why, and he wouldn't say."

"So, he told you to drop everything and run away with him? And you didn't bother to press further?"

"He told me he would explain everything later."

"Surely, you must have suspected something was off?"

"He assured me he didn't kill Eva, and I believed him. He said he was getting framed, and we needed to get out of the country. He said that if I wanted to be with him, I had to come now. I made a decision. But I didn't know that he was going to hijack a plane."

"And you didn't do anything to stop him."

"What could I have done?" she asked, exasperated.

The room was silent for a moment.

"If Jason didn't kill Eva, who did?"

"I don't know."

"Nolan?"

"I don't know. Maybe. Jason never talked about Nolan or his job. All the employees sign strict confidentiality agreements."

"But surely you two talked a little? You trusted each other, right?"

"We didn't talk about Nolan or Eva. The only thing he said to me was that Eva was having an affair with Liam, and that was after it was common knowledge."

"If you know anything, you need to come clean," I said.

"I don't know anything."

I almost felt bad for her. Her life had been ruined over one bad decision to stand by her man. It's unfortunate she chose the wrong man.

"Where did Jason get the fake passports?"

"I don't know."

"He had one for both of you."

"Jason was paranoid. He kept a bug-out bag with supplies, weapons, cash—whatever he thought we'd need in case of an emergency."

"He kept it in a storage facility under an assumed name, right?"

She nodded. "He told me it was in case the world went to hell in a handbasket and we had to get out quickly. I never thought he'd use it in a scenario like this."

"The aircraft was chartered under an assumed name. And the Feds found $100,000 in cash in a duffel bag."

"Like I said, he kept emergency funds on hand." She paused. "Look, if anybody killed Eva, it was Nolan. If Jason had any involvement, it was at Nolan's request. That, I can assure you."

———

42

We didn't have anything tying Nolan to the crime. All we had was an eyewitness who saw Jason loading a similar trunk onto his boat. Nolan was smart enough not to talk to us at this point. We needed something solid to tie him to the murder, and right now, we didn't have it.

A sick feeling rumbled in my stomach that the billionaire would probably get away with it if he had any involvement.

By the time we left the station, JD and I were more than ready to unwind. We swung by the dealership to get the headlights swapped out. It was a pretty simple fix, but cost a fortune. The service advisor wasn't shocked by anything anymore. He just laughed and shook his head, more than happy to take JD's money. "I love what you've done with it."

"I'm thinking of keeping it that way," JD said.

Driving around in a car full of bullet holes certainly created intrigue. We got more stares and attention than ever.

The service department got us in and out, and we headed up to Oyster Avenue and caught happy hour at *Wetsuit*. We ordered a sampler platter and snacked on appetizers while sipping tasty whiskey.

The attempted hijacking was all over the news, and Paris Delaney's beautiful face graced the flatscreen display behind the bar. She'd been blowing up my phone, looking for a comment. I wasn't going to touch this with a 10-foot pole. There was already an uproar on social media, blaming law enforcement for the death of the hostage and saying the shooting of the hijacker was unnecessary. It certainly could have been handled better, and the events were unfortunate.

My phone buzzed with a call from Sophia Breslin. "Looks like you had a rough day."

"I've had better."

"Sorry you lost a hostage."

"I didn't lose a hostage. The Feds lost a hostage. That didn't happen on my watch."

"Well, I've got a little something that might cheer you up. I found Elias Fink. He's on Margarita Island just outside of Porlamar. He's got a little villa on the beach."

"And how do you know this?"

"My source."

"Your source had outdated information before."

"This is updated information. I'll send you pics as of this morning."

Several images buzzed through to my phone—telephoto shots of the infamous terrorist strolling the beach with a particularly attractive young Venezuelan woman.

"Send those to your people," Sophia said. "Verify them."

"I will."

"Then we'll go down and kill him."

"I don't think there's going to be any *we* involved."

"Oh, no. You're not cutting me out of the deal. I want in on the action."

"Isabella will never allow that."

"Unacceptable. I've done nothing but try to earn back your trust and provide you with good intel. I'm going down there with or without you. I prefer backup, but I'll do it myself if I have to. And, as I mentioned, we wipe the slate clean once the job's done. No warrants. My record's clear."

"That's a big ask."

"Isabella can finagle it. She has power and connections."

"We'll see."

"You wouldn't have the intel if it weren't for me. When Elias Fink is dead, the 3-letter agencies will be thanking me. Or, at least, they should be. You know I'm right. Run it by her. See what she says."

I hesitated for a moment. "I'll be in touch."

"I know you will." She ended the call.

I sent the images to Isabella. She called me back 20 minutes later. "The photos don't look manipulated. I'll send an operative I have in the country to do a little recon, see if we can confirm the sighting. I'll also start scanning the cellular networks in the area and see if we can get a voice match. But Elias isn't stupid enough to use a cell phone for anything other than texts." She paused. "What does your gut tell you?"

"I think the only way to confirm is to get eyes on the target. How reliable is your operative?"

"Reliable, but recon only. I can't send him to do the job. He doesn't have the training or the resources. That's where you come in."

"I'm ready when you are. By the way, Sophia wants in on the mission, and she wants a clear reputation afterward. I know what you're gonna say... *hell no.*"

She paused for a moment. "The chatter is increasing. Something is up. Fink is definitely planning another attack."

"Do you have a suspected target?"

"No. But this is big. I'm hearing rumors of nuclear material."

"A dirty bomb?"

"That's what I'm hearing," she said.

"I thought those were considered unlikely due to logistical factors."

"There is the initial hurdle of acquiring nuclear material, but there are a shocking amount of resources available worldwide," Isabella said. "Everything from abandoned Soviet thermal generators to corrupt employees at nuclear labs and universities."

"Then you have to worry about transporting the material and not irradiating yourself in the process."

"True," Isabella said. "But it doesn't mean a few zealots won't try. And if detonated with conventional material, the radioactive damage should be limited, but those in the immediate vicinity of the blast will suffer long-term health problems. The biggest issue is the fear and panic it will create within the American public. And my guess is that's all Fink is really after. He thrives on disruption and chaos."

"Any idea when this is going to go down?"

"No, but I'm working on it."

"What do I tell Sophia?"

"You tell her exactly what she wants to hear."

I lifted a surprised eyebrow.

"Take her with you. She provided good intel so far, albeit a little out of date at times. I think she wants him dead as bad as we do. You are not safe as long as Fink is still in existence. But once the job is done, kill her."

I hesitated.

"You haven't developed a soft spot for her, have you?"

"No."

"Then get rid of her. We'll kill two birds with one stone, so to speak. She's dangerous and a threat. You know that."

I was silent.

"You don't have a problem with that, do you?"

43

We indulged in a few more happy hour specials, then headed to the practice studio.

Crash showed up late and drunk. He reeked of whiskey.

"You forget we had practice?" Styxx snarked when Crash finally entered.

"I'm here, aren't I?" Crash slurred. He stumbled to his bass rig, shouldered his ax, and switched on his amplifier. "I'm ready to rock 'n' roll!" He lifted both hands into the air, making a rock 'n' roll sign and howling.

JD and I exchanged a concerned glance.

"I thought you were going to go easy on the whiskey," I said.

Crash's face crinkled. "I just had a few drinks to loosen up."

His eyes were bloodshot. He had more than a few drinks.

I know, those that live in glass houses shouldn't cast stones. JD and I weren't stone-cold sober either. But we weren't falling down drunk. Not yet.

Crash fumbled through practice, flubbing notes and playing sloppy. It was excusable once in a while, but if this was going to be a regular occurrence, it was unacceptable. More than that, I was concerned for his well-being.

The usual crowd that flooded the studio during practice felt the tension. It was clear *Wild Fury* wasn't firing on all cylinders.

I pulled Crash aside after practice. "Listen, what did we talk about the other day?"

"Why are you hassling me, man?"

"Because I don't want to see the band fall apart."

"It's not going to fall apart," he said, trying to minimize the situation.

"It is if you keep acting this way."

"What way?"

I just shook my head in frustration. "I know you're going through a tough time right now. But don't let it pull you down so far that you can't get back up."

"Chill out. I'm just blowing off a little steam. That's all."

"Well, don't blow it off before practice or before shows. Got it?"

Crash frowned. "What are you gonna do? Fire me? Good luck finding a replacement."

It was an unusual attitude from Crash. He was an easy-going, humble guy. This wasn't typical. I'd never heard him talk that way before.

Crash walked away from me, done listening to anything I had to say.

I exchanged a glance with the rest of the guys as Crash pushed out of the rehearsal space and into the hallway.

"I think it's time we consider a backup plan," Styxx said. He raised his hands innocently. "That's all I'm saying."

"There is no Wild Fury without the four of us," Dizzy said. "There is no backup plan. We did the whole *stand-in bass player* thing once, and it was cool and all, but it wasn't the same."

"He'll snap out of it," JD said. "He just needs a minute. God knows we've all been upside down over a girl before."

JD was no stranger to heartache. With six ex-wives, he'd been through his fair share of it. He moped around for weeks after Sloan dumped him, and she was only a *prospective* number seven.

I found Crash outside, blazing a joint with the usual miscreants that hung out by the entrance.

"How did you get up here?" I asked him.

"I drove."

"Come on, we'll give you a ride home."

"I don't need a ride home."

"Yes, you do."

"I don't want to go home."

"We'll make sure he gets home okay," one of the miscreants said.

He didn't look like the epitome of responsibility.

"Give me your keys," I said to Crash.

His face twisted.

"Hand them over." My tone was non-negotiable.

He frowned, then dug a reluctant hand into his pocket and fished them out. They jingled as he slapped them into my palm. The keys had inadvertently latched onto a small white glassine paper baggie in Crash's pocket, and it tumbled to the ground.

My eyes narrowed. I knew exactly what it was.

I reached down and scooped it up, my jaw tight, my eyes on fire. The glossy, translucent paper was stamped with the logo of a rocket ship and the phrase *Blast Off*. It contained an off-white powder. "What the hell is this?"

44

Crash shrugged. "I don't know."

My face tensed. I dangled the baggie of heroin in front of his face. "It fell out of your pocket."

"No it didn't."

"I saw it."

"It's not mine."

"Then you won't mind when I do this," I said. I tore open the bag and emptied it. The white powder drifted away with the breeze.

Crash's eyes rounded.

"Where did you get it from?"

"I told you, that wasn't mine."

I looked at the miscreants, my angry eyes blazing into them. "If any one of you sold this to him, it's your ass."

"Don't look at me, man," a miscreant said. "We just say no to drugs."

"Empty your pockets. Everybody. Now!"

They all exchanged uneasy glances."

"I'm not playing around with you. Turn them out," I growled.

The rock 'n' rollers reluctantly complied, pulling out the pockets of their skinny jeans.

The impromptu search turned up a couple of joints, cigarettes, loose change, lots of lint, and a few pills here and there, but no heroin.

"See, we're clean," another miscreant said.

I wasn't going to hassle them about the marijuana. The DA had stopped prosecuting personal use amounts.

I turned my attention back to Crash. "Where did it come from?"

Crash sighed and finally admitted, "It was Faye's. She left it at the apartment."

I shook my head. "I searched the apartment the other night."

"Well, maybe you didn't look hard enough."

My jaw flexed, and I stared him down. "You don't even know what's in this stuff," I cautioned.

He shrugged again.

"You don't know what it's cut with. It could be heroin mixed with fentanyl. There could have been enough in that baggie to kill you and everybody else here. Is that what you want? Are you looking for a way out?"

"No, man." He paused for a moment, and his eyes filled. "I'm just tired of hurting."

A tear rolled down his cheek.

It broke my heart to see Crash like this. I pulled him away from the miscreants and calmly asked, "How long have you been using the stuff?"

He shrugged. "I'm not really using, man. I just dabbled here and there. And I only smoke it. I never put anything in my veins."

I deflated and exhaled a long breath. "It's okay. We all make mistakes. We all make bad choices."

"I'm sorry. I know I let you down."

"You'll let me down if you keep doing it. I think it's time we talk about getting you into a program."

His face crinkled. "I don't need a program. I swear. I'm not an addict. I'm not an alcoholic."

I looked at him with skeptical eyes.

"Like you said. I just made some bad choices. That's all. I'm not going to make any more bad choices."

I kept staring at him.

"I swear. I'm never touching that stuff again. No more drinking before practice. But you can't tell me I can't drink after. No way."

"Hop in the car. We'll take you home."

He shifted, then finally nodded. "What about my ride? It could get stolen in the lot overnight."

I looked over at his car. Let's just say it wasn't the belle of the ball. "Trust me. No one's gonna take your car. Jump in with JD, and I'll drive it back to your apartment."

He nodded, and I patted him on the back as he walked with JD toward the Porsche.

I ambled across the lot to his beat-up white four-door and climbed into the driver's seat. The door creaked as I pulled it shut. I twisted the ignition, put it into gear, and followed JD back to Crash's apartment.

We hung out for a while, ordered in Chinese takeout, and took another cursory glance around to make sure he wasn't holding any other illicit substances.

Part of me wanted to check Crash into rehab that night. But he could just walk out of there at any time. I knew from experience that nobody ever got clean who didn't want to. Everybody had to come to that moment of *enlightenment* themselves. The moment when you realize that continuing down the path is going to lead to an untimely demise. And unfortunately, it can take a long time to hit bottom and come to that realization.

45

The smell of Italian seasonings filled the air when I stepped aboard the *Avventura*. Buddy greeted me excitedly and then darted into the galley leading me to my visitor.

Sophia was in the galley, cooking.

"I didn't realize you were so domesticated," I said.

"There's a lot of things about me that you don't realize. I made you some lasagna."

I had to admit, it smelled good. "You've lost your mind if you think I'm going to eat anything you serve me."

A lascivious smirk curled her plump lips. "Well, if you won't eat my lasagna, there's something else you can eat that won't kill you."

I ignored her. "What are you doing here?"

"Can't a girl cook a man dinner every once in a while? Or is that against the rules?"

"I didn't think you played by the rules."

"I don't."

"I want my tender back."

"It's back. It's tied up a few slips down. I'll take a cab when I leave."

"When are you leaving?"

"Take a bite of my lasagna and tell me it's not the best you've ever had. Then I'll leave."

I gave her a skeptical glance.

She sighed and rolled her eyes. "How many opportunities have I had to kill you or let you die? Do you really think I would have gone to the trouble of cooking lasagna, which took me several hours to do, if I wanted you dead?"

She had a point.

She put on oven mitts, pulled the pan out of the oven, and set it on a pad on the counter. She proceeded to carve up squares and transfer them onto plates and brought them to the dining nook. She poured two glasses of red wine and brought them to the table. She slid into the seat and lifted her glass. "Are you going to join me, or are you going to make me eat alone?"

I reluctantly slid into the bench seat across from her.

She lifted her glass to toast. "To killing Elias Fink."

That was something I could certainly toast to.

We clinked glasses, and I sipped the wine. If she was going to kill me, she'd been rather inefficient about it as of late.

She took a bite of her lasagna.

I switched plates, taking hers.

She rolled her eyes.

I shoveled a bite into my mouth, and it was an explosion of garlic, onions, tomatoes, pasta, and cheesy goodness. The red sauce was zesty, tangy, and sweet. The ground beef was juicy.

Sophia watched eagerly, awaiting my opinion. "Is it not the best?"

I took another bite and let the delightful taste soak my buds. I washed it down with a sip of wine. "It's not the worst."

She frowned at me. "Go ahead, say it. You know it's true."

"Okay. It's pretty damn good."

"Pretty good?"

"Alright, it's better than pretty good."

She groaned. "I guess I'll settle for that." She took another bite. "Have you heard back from Isabella?"

"She's attempting to verify your intel."

"I assure you, it's accurate and up-to-date. What did she say about me going along?"

I hesitated. "She said it's my call."

Sophia smiled. "And how are you going to call it?"

"Well, after lasagna like this, how can I say no?"

"Yay! We are a team."

I ate the lasagna and drank the wine. By the time I scraped the last of it from my plate, I was pretty certain that I wasn't going to die. At least not from the lasagna.

Sophia cleared the table, rinsed the dishes in the sink, and put them in the dishwasher. I gave her a hand cleaning up the galley.

She grabbed the bottle of wine and refilled our glasses.

"So, what do we do now?" she asked, her sultry eyes locked on mine.

"The man you claim killed Quinn... Where is his body?"

"Do you really want to know? Will that give you confidence in me?"

"Isabella says he hasn't turned up on the circuit since Quinn's death."

"And he won't."

"So, where are the remains?"

"Let's not talk business. Not now. Surely there are other things you'd rather do?" she asked with a lustful sparkle in her eyes, inching closer.

She set her wine on the counter, dropped to her knees, and fumbled with the waistband of my shorts.

Call me weak, but what was I supposed to do?

46

The lasagna was good, but the dessert was better.

My God, could she give good *dessert*.

We played around in the galley, whipping up a few more delights, then retired to my stateroom where we gave the mattress a workout. We definitely burned a few calories and ended up a sweaty mess.

Best cardio routine ever.

Afterward, she lay beside me, stroking my chest with her delicate fingers. "See, that wasn't so bad, was it?"

"I've had worse."

She smacked me playfully. "And you're still alive. I'd call that a win-win. Of course, you could go back to hating me, or we could go for another round."

It was tempting. I was about to take her up on the offer when my phone buzzed on the nightstand. I almost ignored it, but I thought better of it. I grabbed the phone and looked at the screen—it was Isabella.

"What have you got?" I asked.

"Eyes on the target. We need to move ASAP."

I sat up. "Really?"

Sophia hung onto my every word.

"There will be a Skymax King C350 XR waiting for you at the Coconut Key FBO in 30 minutes."

"We're going tonight?"

"No time like the present. Unless you want me to find someone else."

"No. I'm all about it."

"Now for the bad news."

I cringed.

"We have zero operational support on this one. If things go wrong, you're on your own. The three-letter agencies and the US government will deny any involvement. Is that clear?"

"Isn't that always the way?"

"For a host of reasons, they don't want to touch this right now."

"Even though Fink may be plotting something," I said in an incredulous tone.

"The politics of it are above my pay grade. I was told to let sleeping dogs lie. But I'm not about to let that bastard get away because some politician is worried about re-election."

"You'd think taking out one of the most wanted terrorists in the world would be good for business."

"Remember, we live in crazy world where up is down and day is night. In the current climate, I don't think anyone wants blood on their hands, especially if something goes wrong."

"Nothing is going to go wrong," I said, full of optimism.

"Just don't look for any outside assistance. There is no cavalry coming if the shit hits the fan."

"Understood."

"You and your team will make a HALO jump. You'll hit the beach before dawn, storm the compound, and take out the target. Get proof of death and a DNA sample if you can."

"Copy."

"When you accomplish your mission objective, I'll have a chopper take you to Trinidad & Tobago. From there I've arranged a flight back. You will be given weapons, clothing, and fake passports at the FBO before your departure. Like I said, if anything goes wrong, no one will claim you. This is all or nothing. Are you sure you want to do this?"

"I suppose a drone strike is out of the question."

"That's a can of worms. Besides, I know you want to get up close and personal, anyway."

"Fink certainly has it coming."

"Yes, he does." Isabella paused. "And the other thing we discussed... You're on board, right?"

I glanced at Sophia. "We are ready to do this."

47

I called Jack and told him *Operation Deadly Venom* was a go. He swung by the marina and picked us up. Sophia climbed into the back of the Porsche, and we zipped across the island to the FBO.

We parked in the lot and hustled through the terminal. I left my weapons and ID on the *Avventura*. We weren't going to take anything that could be tracked back to us. This was a black-op in every sense of the word.

The matte gray SkyMax King sat on the tarmac, waiting for us. It was a multimission twin-engine aircraft with a wing span of 57 feet. It could hold 15 people and had a maximum takeoff weight of 17,000 pounds. With a cruising speed of 327 nautical miles an hour, and a range of nearly 3,000 miles, we could be over the drop site in as little as 4.5 hours.

The beauty of the SkyMax was its altitude ceiling at 35,000 feet. I figured we'd make the HALO (High Altitude Low Opening) jump around 22,000'. It would simplify things to a degree. Though, there was nothing simple about a HALO jump. Of course, we'd need supplemental oxygen at that level and would pre-breathe 100% oxygen during the ascent to altitude to purge nitrogen. We planned on 22,000 feet, but wanted to be prepared if circumstances necessitated a higher approach. Without pure oxygen, a quick ascent to could result in the formation of nitrogen bubbles, giving you the bends in a similar fashion to divers that surface too fast. *Not a good thing when jumping out of an airplane.*

Since the air was thinner, you fell faster and had a higher maximum terminal velocity until you reached denser air.

It was a hell of a rush.

We were greeted on the tarmac by a pilot, copilot, and physiology tech whose names I cannot mention. The tech would monitor us for impairment caused by the altitude prior to the jump.

We boarded the plane and were issued our gear—all of it Russian-made. The jungle camo, the thermal knit underwear (it's cold at 22,000 feet), the parachutes, the jump helmets, the goggles, the supplemental oxygen canisters, the folding stock 7.62mm AK-103s, and the sidearms. Our passports were Russian as well.

If we got caught, the subterfuge wouldn't fool anybody. It was just an added bit of misdirection. Nobody would have to explain how a team of rogue assassins acquired US military issued weapons. The only items that weren't Russian-made were the iPhones with satellite sleeves and bluetooth earbuds that would allow encrypted team communications via Cobra Company's satellite, *CobraNet™*.

The cargo area of the SkyMax was empty—just a few spartan jump-seats with canvas-webbed backing.

The Pratt & Whitney engines rumbled to life, and the plane taxied to the runway.

I suited up in my tactical gear, checked my AK and magazines, and examined the Starikov SRX-M2 semi-automatic pistol. It had an 18-round magazine and fired Russian-made body armor-piercing rounds. A favorite of Russian Spetsnaz and Special Forces. Extremely effective in close-quarter combat, but they'd lose their velocity quickly and had a limited range.

The pistol felt good in my hand and had a nice balance. I pulled the slide and loaded a cartridge into the chamber with a satisfying clack, then holstered the weapon.

The pilot throttled up, and the engines howled. The aircraft lumbered forward, gaining speed, the fuselage vibrating. With a pull of the controls, the craft nosed up and climbed into the night sky.

I glanced through the circular window at the ground below, the lights of Coconut Key flickering.

It was just after 11 PM.

Sophia and JD examined their equipment.

I did a safety check of my chute and supplemental oxygen. When I was satisfied that everything was in order, I connected to the onboard oxygen—the cabin wasn't pressurized.

I studied the satellite photos of the compound that Isabella had sent me. Afterward, I leaned back and closed my eyes.

48

There was a lot of hurry up and wait in the military. You learned to sleep on command, grabbing moments when and where you could. The four hours of sleep during the flight was much needed.

JD nudged me awake. "We're getting close."

I peeled open my eyes, did a final check of the gear, and prepared myself for the adventure. The PT checked our cognitive function when we were at altitude. Hypoxia can cause all kinds of problems.

I put the noise-canceling wireless earbuds into my ear. They allowed normal speech frequencies through but attenuated high decibel sounds, offering hearing protection in combat environments. The earbuds were already paired to the phones and ready to go. Isabella had set us up well.

We all launched a networking app on the phones and joined a private password-protected chat group Isabella had created for us. She would be able to hear and monitor our comms, and we could communicate directly with her in real-time. It was a blend of consumer and military tech with high-end encryption and security. Modern warfare.

Technology was changing the face of special ops. Smart glasses and contact lenses were on the horizon that could identify and track everything within the visual field. Together with biometric sensors, tactical operations centers could monitor the status of troops, identify friends and foes, and get a real-time view of ground-level operations. *There were so many new and interesting ways to kill people.*

I designated myself as Bravo 1, JD as Bravo 2, and Sophia as Bravo 3.

"I don't want to be Bravo 3. I want to be X-ray."

"Why?"

"It sounds cooler."

I rolled my eyes. "Fine. You're X-ray."

"I want to be Whiskey Tango Foxtrot," JD said.

"You're Bravo 2," I said.

He frowned at me.

"Radio check, over," Sophia said.

"Check," JD replied.

"Check," I said.

"Hello, my lovelies," Isabella said, her voice crackling in my ear. "It's your Guardian Angel speaking."

"And you do sound angelic, if I do say so myself," JD said, ever the smooth talker.

"Flattery will get you everywhere, Bravo 2."

"Isabella, I don't believe you've met Sophia Breslin," I said.

"Not in person, but her reputation precedes her."

"I'm working toward revamping my image," Sophia said.

"Impress me," Isabella said.

"I'm working on that."

We sat back and waited for the moment to arrive.

HALO jumps were not for the faint of heart. Between 2011 and 2016, 11 Special Operators died during HALO training jumps. There were a lot of things that could go wrong. The added gear could destabilize your descent. Chutes could open improperly or not at all. Your oxygen mask could get ripped off during the jump. The last thing you wanted was to suffer hypoxia. Nothing worse than losing consciousness during a jump and being unable to open your parachute. Jumps at 28,000 to 30,000 feet were common and required more caution. More time at altitude, and more to go wrong. We weren't crazy high at 22,000 feet, but high enough. The air at 22,000 feet is roughly -28° Celsius. Not a pleasant temperature. If you don't want frostbite, gloves and polypropylene knit undergarments are a must.

I donned my helmet, gloves, and goggles, then switched from the onboard oxygen to the supplemental.

JD slid open the jump door as we streaked through the clouds. We hovered in position near the exit until the pilot gave us the thumbs up. When he did, I gave a last look to Sophia and JD, then jumped out of a perfectly good aircraft.

I plummeted through the thin air, wind whistling around my helmet. I was on top of the world, literally. I felt like I could reach up and touch the stars.

JD and Sophia followed after me.

My heart pounded, and adrenaline pumped through my veins. This was better than any cup of coffee.

My fellow comrades joined me on the way down.

A slight smirk curled my lips. It was hard not to enjoy this part of the adventure. This was the *fun and games* part. The part where you were along for the ride. There was no getting back in the plane now. Win, lose, or draw, *Operation Deadly Venom* was in motion.

The flickering lights of Porlamar grew closer. What started as a tiny speck below grew in size.

The world certainly looked different from up here. Detached and removed. Despite blazing toward the ground at a lethal speed, I had a Zen-like calmness about me. All of the politics and chaos of the world vanished for a moment. I was just a guy flying through the heavens, and the world below me was just a rock hurtling through space.

The Earth was both vast and small at the same time. All of the man-made conflict seemed trivial. A view like this reminded me just how small and insignificant I was in the scheme of the Universe. How inconsequential all the power struggles could be on the larger timeline.

The giant orb below me was a swirl of blue, green, and brown. It had been in existence for 6 billion years and had another 6 billion to go. In the scheme of things, does anything we do really matter?

I was oddly philosophical as I free-fell toward the ground, preparing to kill a man.

A bad, bad man.

We cut it close to the wire and deployed our chutes at sub-2000 feet. The fabric unfurled, abruptly slowing my descent, yanking me against the harness.

That was the first hurdle—chute successfully opened. *Score bonus points.*

And that's where philosophy ended, and danger began.

49

We glided down through the black sky. The waves crashed against the shore a thousand feet below my boots. I watched the ground rush to greet me as I touched down in the soft sand. I instantly released my harness.

"Son-of-a-bitch!" JD howled as he landed beside me an instant later.

He tumbled to the ground and released his harness. He clutched his ankle. His face tensed, the veins in his temple bulging. His skin reddened as he held in the pain.

I cringed and rushed to his aid. "Can you walk it off?"

"I guess we're about to find out."

I grabbed his arm and hoisted him from the sand.

JD took a step, then crumpled again, his face tensed with pain.

I helped him hobble up the shore and deposited him in a clump of foliage.

Sophia had touched down and wadded up our chutes. She carried them up to the bushes and dumped them.

I looked up and down the beach. There wasn't a soul out at this hour. The distant lights of Porlamar flickered. As far as I could tell, we made our landing undetected.

"Do we abort?" Sophia asked.

"Hell no!" JD grumbled.

"This might be our only shot," I said.

"I'll be fine," JD assured. "I just need a minute to shake it off."

I knelt down and examined his ankle. I was no doctor, but I knew my way around field injuries. I manipulated the joint and pressed on a ligament.

JD almost went through the roof. He bit his tongue and took the pain, his face beet red.

"Does that hurt?" I teased.

"Fuck you!"

"You tore a ligament. Sit this one out."

"To hell with that."

I gave him a stern gaze. "You're gonna sit here and provide overwatch. You got me? Otherwise the mission is compromised."

JD frowned but nodded.

"We'll pick you up on the way out."

We left him in the bushes and advanced down a path covered by a canopy of trees. It led to a small oceanside villa. The structure had white stucco walls and orange Spanish tile on the roof. It was surrounded by an 8-foot perimeter wall.

We held up on the path, taking cover to the side in the underbrush. My eyes scanned through the trees, scoping out the perimeter wall, looking for cameras or guards.

I lowered my night vision opticals and continued to scan the area. "Guardian Angel, Bravo 1, over?" I whispered.

I waited for Isabella to reply. There was nothing but static in my ear.

"Bravo 2, status update," I said.

"Situation normal," JD replied.

The air was thick with humidity, and crickets chirped. Stars flickered above, and mosquitoes buzzed about in the underbrush.

"Guardian Angel, Bravo 1, do you copy?"

"Copy. Lost signal for a moment. What's the matter with Bravo 2?"

"Rough landing," I said. "Proceeding as a two-person unit."

"Copy."

"Do you have eyes on the compound?" I asked.

"Affirmative," Isabella replied, watching the satellite footage. "I see no movement. You are safe to proceed."

"Copy," I said.

Sophia and I advanced toward the perimeter wall. I gave her a hand as she climbed over. I scaled the wall behind her and silently dropped down to the other side. We huddled in the shrubbery, scoping out the courtyard. There was a nice swimming pool with several lounge chairs on the patio, along with a table underneath an umbrella. The area was well manicured.

This type of luxury was not typical. Fink's relationship with the regime, combined with wealth acquired through weapons and drug trafficking, allowed him an opulent life-style while most lived in squalor.

The lights were out inside the house, and I saw no movement. No guards walking the perimeter. For an international terrorist, Fink was lax on security.

"Guardian Angel, Bravo 1. You see any movement?"

"You are the only two I see."

"Are we sure the target is at the location?"

"We are not sure of anything."

Sophia and I advanced along the shrubbery to the back of the house, moving past the tiki hut poolside bar. Large windows offered a view from the living room to the pool. French doors opened to a second-story terrace that covered the back patio.

It was an unusually cool night for the region, with the temperature in the mid 70s. One of the French doors on the terrace was open, allowing the gentle breeze in, rustling the sheer white curtains.

The stucco walls were rough, coated with uneven swipes of aggregate, making it look like the surface of a choppy sea. The ridges were just deep enough for a finger and toe hold.

I peered through the patio windows with my night vision and didn't see a soul in the living room. I was beginning to think that Elias had moved on or been given a heads up.

Sophia kept a watch on the perimeter.

I lifted the goggles, and with my rifle slung across my back, I grabbed hold of a ridge on the stucco. I pulled on it to assess its strength. The mixture of concrete, aggregate, and sand seemed solid. I reached another hand up and grabbed another ridge, then found a toe hold and started climbing up the side of the house. Bits of concrete and sand crumbled away underneath my feet with each step.

Sophia stayed on the ground with her weapon shouldered, scanning the area for threats.

Isabella crackled in my ear, "Bravo 1, I've lost visual. There's interference with the satellite."

"Copy that."

I continued my ascent, then inched sideways toward the balcony. I grabbed hold of the railing and climbed over. I was on the terrace in no time.

I swung my weapon around, lowered my night vision, and approached the French door. I held up in the doorway and angled the barrel of my rifle into the bedroom. There was a king bed with nightstands on either side and a dresser on the opposite wall. Above it, a flatscreen TV. The master bathroom was to my left, and at the far wall was the entrance to the bedroom.

Elias Fink wasn't here.

I crept forward into the bedroom, then quietly stepped into the master bath and cleared the area.

"You see anything?" Isabella asked.

"Negative," I said in a barely audible breath.

I stepped back into the bedroom, checked underneath the bed, then moved to the master closet. The door was closed. Closed doors were always a source of tension.

I lowered the rifle and drew my pistol for better mobility. I reached a hand out, twisted the knob, and pulled the door open quietly.

It creaked ever so slightly.

I winced at the sound.

There was no one hiding in the closet.

I edged toward the bedroom door and held up at the corner. I listened intently for noises, but all I could hear was the pounding of my own heart.

I swung the barrel of my pistol around the corner and pushed into the hallway, clearing both directions. There was a banister that overlooked the foyer on the first floor. Down the hallway to my left was another guest bedroom and a staircase that spiraled down to the foyer. To my right, there was another wing that housed another bedroom and a lounge area. It was a nice home. A little oasis by the sea.

"Give me a sitrep, Bravo 1," Sophia said.

I said nothing and crept down the hallway toward the guest bedroom to my left. I moved slowly. Fortunately, the home was floored in saltillo tile, which eliminated any squeaky floorboards—always a hazard when doing second-story work.

"Bravo 2, status update," Sophia said.

There was no response from JD either.

I reached the end of the hallway and hovered by the door to the guest bedroom. It was slightly ajar. I pushed it open just wide enough to slip through. I swept the barrel across the corners, clearing the room. Then inched toward the closet and cleared it as well. The room was empty and so was the guest bath.

"Still no sign of the target," I whispered.

"Copy," Sophia said. "I'm still in position."

I moved back into the hallway and headed to the north wing, moving past the staircase. I angled my pistol over the banister, down toward the foyer, scanning the area.

"Bravo 2, do you copy?" Sophia said.

Still no response from JD.

"Guardian Angel, do you have eyes again?" Sophia asked.

"Negative."

An increasing sense of dread filled me as I inched through the darkness, approaching the other wing. I moved past the lounge toward the other guest bedroom. I grabbed the doorknob and twisted, easing it open. I swept the barrel of my pistol across the room and again saw nothing.

I checked the closet and underneath the bed. There was officially no one on the second floor of the house. I hadn't seen anyone through the windows below. I was beginning to think the mission was a bust when a familiar voice crackled in my ear. "So, you finally came to visit?"

My heart sank. I'd recognize Elias Fink's voice anywhere. The fact that he was speaking to me over our encrypted comm channel was highly disturbing.

"Well, you sent so many assassins my way, I thought I'd return the favor," I said.

"How's that working out for you?"

"Not very well at the moment."

"I'd say. You and your friend need to drop your weapons and give yourselves up, or your friend with the gimp leg dies."

50

F ink's goons swarmed the compound. My first thought was that Sophia had set us up. Seemed like a lot of trouble to go to, but here we were.

That thought quickly vanished when a goon dragged her inside the house with a gun to her head.

I lowered my weapon and set it on the floor, then descended the steps with my hands up as the goons aimed automatic rifles at me.

They dragged JD into the house, hobbling along—and they weren't too gentle about it. He winced with pain.

Elias appeared, wearing shorts and a T-shirt. He was in his mid 40s and clean-cut with a day's worth of stubble. He had short brown hair and brown eyes and had kept himself fit over the years. He didn't fit the mold for the typical international terrorist. He could have been a doctor, lawyer, or tech guru in Silicon Valley. But instead, he chose to sow the seeds of anarchy across the globe, and he'd been doing it since his early 20s.

He could make the argument that he was doing it to force political change, to liberate the oppressed, to fight against imperialism, or whatever. But the truth of the matter was that he just liked to create chaos. Some people are just angry and full of hate.

I found that most people are full of contradictions. It's part of the human condition. Elias had been associated with numerous terrorist organizations over the years. He had falling outs with some, forged new alliances with others, and formed his own group, Sector Underground. But in retrospect, it seemed like a haphazard reign of terror. And there was big money in assisting terrorist organizations, providing weapons, consulting, and logistics. Many organizations were funded by the trafficking of illicit drugs, human trafficking, weapons, ransomware, and other schemes.

"This was both bold and stupid," Fink said. "I have no doubt that the witch at Cobra Company is behind this?"

I said nothing.

"Matters not. What's important is that you are here, and we have a chance to catch up. I didn't have that luxury with the other members of your team. I'm going to look forward to watching you die a slow and painful death."

My jaw tightened.

"I know it's not going to bring my brother back, but it will make me feel better."

Fink's brother had been killed during a hostage rescue. I led the team, and Fink blamed me.

"Maybe if you hadn't engaged in this lifestyle, your brother would still be alive," I said.

"Is this the part where you tell me you were just doing your job? Do you know how many atrocities are committed across the globe in the name of *"Just doing my job?"* The world would be a different place if people stood up and refused to do the unconscionable things dictated to them by their government."

"I guess you get a pass for kidnapping and terror?"

I don't think he particularly liked being called out on it. "I am just a reflection of your world. I didn't create this mess. I'm only responding to it. As long as there is imperialism and injustice, there will be people like me fighting against it."

"So, you're a crusader?"

"I am a light in a sea of darkness."

I rolled my eyes. "Maybe you should seek therapy."

He laughed. "Trust me, my line of work is very therapeutic."

"And detonating a dirty bomb is somehow fighting oppression and injustice?"

His face tensed. He drew close, and his narrow eyes stared into mine. "All I can do is be the catalyst for change."

"Terrorizing innocent people is a catalyst?"

"The people are far from innocent. They are all complicit. My actions will cause people to stop and think. It will wake people up from their coma. They'll slip back into it shortly —they always do. But for a brief moment, they might contemplate the nature of their existence, and the atrocities perpetrated by their government."

"You know what I think?"

His curious eyes surveyed me.

"I think that's all a load of bullshit. You just like to blow stuff up."

He considered my statement for a moment. "You may be right." He flashed a smarmy smile. "Either way, my plan is in motion, and you can't do anything to stop it."

"What are you targeting?"

He smirked. "That is for me to know and for you to never find out."

"What are you so worried about? It's not like any of us are getting out of here alive."

"I'm glad you've accepted your fate."

The only thing that I had accepted was my renewed determination to rid the planet of the scumbag before he could cause further harm.

My eyes glanced from JD to Sophia. Dread tensed her face, and her wide eyes flicked about the room, surveying the goons and the situation.

Fink turned his attention to her and stepped closer. "And you, my dear, have betrayed my trust. You failed to complete a task which you were paid to do. To make matters worse, you actively worked against me. You killed a man that I had hired to do the same job." Fink frowned and shook his head. "There's nothing I value more than loyalty.

And sadly, that word doesn't seem to be in your vocabulary."

"I give my loyalty to those who are worthy of it," Sophia said with a defiant stare.

"You should never have taken the job if you didn't intend to complete it. I understand that Deputy Wild can be very charming. But I expected more from a professional such as yourself. You destroyed your reputation."

"I'm so glad you're concerned about it."

Fink held out his hand, palm up. One of his goons placed a black semiautomatic pistol in his grasp. He gripped the pistol and placed the weapon against Sophia's forehead.

The goons holding her arms made sure they were clear of the barrel.

Sophia's eyes rounded.

"While you might not care about your reputation, I care about mine. No one betrays me and lives."

His finger wrapped tight around the trigger, ready to squeeze.

51

I was expecting a loud bang, followed by an unsightly rearrangement of the contents of Sophia's skull.

The situation looked grim. Two thugs held onto Sophia. Two goons attended to me. And two goons surrounded JD.

They were all armed with pistols. Rough and tumble-looking guys that were no strangers to violence and prison cells.

Fink lowered his pistol, and I breathed a momentary sigh of relief. "On second thought, I don't want to clean up the mess." He surveyed Sophia for a moment. "Take her outside and drown her in the pool."

The two goons dragged Sophia toward the patio door. She struggled, kicking and screaming, cussing up a storm, coming up with colorful names for the terrorists.

Fink turned his attention back to me. "I don't know if you care about her or not, but I figured I'd let you watch her die. Then I'll figure out what to do with the two of you."

My body tensed, and my eyes blazed into him.

My judgment regarding Sophia had become cloudy, to say the least. She wasn't all bad. But she wasn't all good either. Nobody really is. We are all shades of gray when you get down to it, though some of us are grayer than others.

Isabella wanted Sophia dead. But the girl had saved my life more than a few times. When it came down to it, I didn't know if I could pull the trigger myself. But that choice was about to get taken away from me.

If there was anything I learned about Sophia, it was never to underestimate her.

The two goons forced her to the edge of the pool. One of them grabbed her by the hair and shoved her head down. They were trying to get her on her knees and plunge her head under by the edge of the pool.

Sophia wasn't having any of it.

She twisted around and roundhoused the goon to her right, kicking him in the back with enough force to splash him into the pool. The big ogre sent a tidal wave rippling.

Like a lightning bolt, Sophia jammed her elbow into the other goon's rib cage. He crumpled around her elbow. Then she twisted around and put a solid fist into his kidney. The blow made him release the grasp on her hair.

Sophia kicked him in the balls.

His eyes bulged, and he doubled over with pain, looking like he was going to hurl. It was the kind of pain that could make anybody want to toss the contents of their stomach.

She finished with an uppercut to the jaw, tumbling him back. Like a viper she struck, snatching his pistol from his shoulder holster. She pumped two rounds into his chest as the thug fell back into the water, blossoming his shirt red before he submerged.

The other goon had his weapon drawn and aimed it at Sophia. He was about to squeeze the trigger.

Sophia aimed the barrel of her pistol in his direction as he fired.

Muzzle flash flickered, and bullets snapped through the air.

While that was going on, I took the opportunity to strike. I kicked the thug beside me in the knee, snapping his medial collateral ligament. It crunched like celery, and his knee collapsed inward at an unnatural angle. *Healthy knees only bend in one direction.*

He tumbled to the ground.

I spun around and planted an elbow into the back of the goon beside me, and his body wrapped around the strike.

He swung the barrel of his pistol around toward me, and I shoved his forearm toward the ceiling.

The gun went off.

The deafening bank echoed through the living room.

Still holding his forearm, I grabbed the barrel of the pistol and twisted it around, snapping his finger in the trigger guard, stripping the weapon from him.

It took an instant to gain control and take aim. I squeezed two shots into him, spotting his shirt with blood.

He tumbled to the ground, and before the body had settled, I'd taken aim at one of the goons struggling with Jack.

Another two shots put that thug down.

Jack and the other thug struggled for the goon's pistol.

From the corner of my eye, I saw Elias aim his gun at me.

Everything happened in the blink of an eye.

Outside, the shot fired from the goon in the pool snapped past Sophia's head and embedded in the stucco, spraying bits of debris. She popped off a few rounds into the goon, exploding his head, making it look like a watermelon that had been dropped from a 40-story building.

The goon's body fell back into the pool, giving a pinkish hue to the water as blood mixed.

The sun was cresting the horizon, and the once black sky was now more of a mauve color.

Fire spewed from the barrel of Fink's pistol as he blasted two shots at me.

I dove for cover and tumbled to the ground, then rolled on one knee and took aim.

Before I could get my shot off. Fink's chest exploded with two bullets exiting at the level of his heart. Glass had shattered as Sophia fired through the window, hitting the terrorist in the back. He fell forward, smacking the saltillo tile, and his weapon clattered away.

She'd saved my ass once again.

I whipped the barrel of my pistol toward the last remaining goon that struggled with Jack. I had a clear shot and took it.

My pistol hammered against my palm, and the sharp smell of gunpowder hung in the air. My bullet hit the thug in his left arm and spun him around. He twisted to the ground just as JD stripped the weapon from his grasp.

The goon fell to the ground and groaned, still alive. He clutched at the wound, blood seeping between his fingers.

"I almost had the situation under control," JD assured me.

He aimed his weapon at the thug writhing on the ground.

I checked the bodies of the nearby thugs for vitals, then advanced to Elias Fink. With my fingertips on his neck, I quickly determined that his reign of terror was over. But I had no doubt that his most recent plot was still in effect. And I still didn't know the target.

52

"Tell me what the target is?" I said, hovering over the last living goon, my weapon aimed at his head.

Sweat misted his skin, and pain grimaced his face. He clutched at his wounded shoulder, trying to stop the tide of blood from seeping onto the tile. "I don't know nothing."

"Bullshit! Tell me where the dirty bomb is going to go off."

"I don't know. I just work security here. I swear," he said through clenched teeth.

"I'm going to put a bullet in both of your kneecaps if you don't start talking," I said. "If you think your shoulder hurts, just wait."

Fear rounded his eyes.

"I swear, I don't know anything."

"Stop lying to me."

"I'm not lying. Fink never told us the details."

"Shoot him in the dick," Sophia said casually. "He'll start talking."

The goon's eyes widened. He looked at her, then back to me. "Keep her away from me, man. She's psycho."

"You'd better start talking," I said.

Sophia stepped to him and aimed her pistol at his crotch.

She meant business.

Panic bathed the goon's face. "Okay, okay! I'll tell you everything I know."

We lorded over the scumbag as he grimaced and moaned.

"Start talking," I demanded.

"I don't know the exact target, but I know he's planning to detonate the bomb in Coconut Key."

"Why Coconut Key?"

"I don't know."

"I'm getting trigger-happy," Sophia said, tightening her grasp.

"Elias wanted to detonate the bomb right under your nose," the thug said.

"When?"

"Sometime today."

"Give me the exact target."

"I don't know."

I gave him a swift kick in the bloody shoulder. He screamed with agony, and his eyes filled with tears. "I swear, I don't know!"

I found the earbuds and sat-phones that Fink had confiscated and attempted to contact Isabella. "Guardian Angel, do you copy?"

"I thought I'd lost an operator for a moment," she replied.

"I'm still here."

"How's the situation?"

"Objective accomplished. We need immediate exfiltration. JD is wounded."

"I've got a helicopter inbound now, flying in under the radar. I can have you all to a landing strip and on a plane and back to Coconut Key within six hours."

"Coconut Key is the target," I said.

"Where?"

I pondered it for a moment. "The Energy Trade Conference. That has to be the target."

"The conference is at the Seven Seas."

"Notify DHS and the FBI. I'll contact the sheriff."

"Do you know when?"

"Sometime today."

"Is there anyone else listening on this channel?" Isabella asked.

"No."

"Have you taken care of your little friend?"

I glanced across the room at Sophia. I knew better than to lie to Isabella. She'd find out the truth anyway. Once trust is broken, it's almost impossible to earn back. "We'll discuss that later."

"For Christ's sake, Tyson. Don't tell me you went soft on her?"

"Not everything is as it seems," I said.

I used the sat-phone to call the sheriff and update him, then we rounded up the weapons and policed our brass. I snapped photos of Elias Fink's bloody body and swabbed a blood sample. I put it in a plastic collection vial that I had carried along and stuffed it into my pocket.

Sophia and I helped JD hobble toward the patio door.

"What about me?" the thug asked, still writhing in agony. "You can't just leave me like this."

"Would you prefer a bullet?" Sophia asked.

He shook his head.

"Call an ambulance," she said to him.

He scoffed. "You can't get an ambulance around here. And hospitals barely have any supplies."

"Maybe you should have thought about that before you started doing terrorist shit," Sophia said.

"I'm just security, man."

"Guardian Angel, Bravo 1... can you send a medic?"

"For whom?" Isabella replied.

"We have a survivor."

"You want to give care to the enemy?"

"See what you can do?"

"I lined up some freelancers in case you got into trouble. Maybe I can arrange something."

"How thoughtful."

"What's the guy's condition?"

"He's stable-ish." I gave the details of the injury.

"I'll send someone to the house. Might be a while."

I told the thug help was on the way and to keep pressure on the wound.

With an arm around each of our shoulders, JD hopped along as we rushed onto the patio and down the path to the beach.

Morning rays of sun cast long shadows, and the amber ball hung just over the horizon, glimmering the water.

The unmistakable patter of rotor blades thumped in the distance, drawing ever closer.

Some early birds on the beach prepared for a day in the sun, setting out towels and lotioning up their skin.

The black helicopter came into view, the rotors a blur. It was flying nap of the earth, hovering only a few feet over the surface of the water—far below radar capabilities. The bird touched down in the soft sand, and we hopped in through the passenger door. The bird lifted into the air, banked around, and headed back in the direction it came.

The commercial pilot was a local from Trinidad and Tobago that Isabella had hired, no doubt paying him a handsome sum to pick us up and keep his mouth shut.

We dumped the weapons over the ocean.

It was a short flight to the neighboring island, and the helicopter pilot dropped us off at the South Terminal of the Piarco International Airport.

The South Terminal handled cargo, general aviation, military, and helicopter operations. There were plenty of helicopter flights to offshore oil rigs, so our arrival in a Bell 407 wasn't anything out of the ordinary. The newer North Terminal was the main passenger terminal that handled commercial flights.

Isabella must have greased a few palms because no one gave us any grief. The matte gray SkyMax King waited for us on the tarmac, refueled and ready to go. We hopped on board, and it wasn't long before we were cleared for takeoff. The engines rumbled, and the craft nosed into the air. We were on our way back to Coconut Key to stop a detonation if we could find the bomb.

Hopefully, the island wouldn't be glowing when we landed.

53

It was late afternoon when we arrived in Coconut Key. The SkyMax touched down, and the wheels shrieked with a puff of smoke. We taxied to the terminal, and the engines wound down.

JD had gone through several instant cold packs from the med kit to reduce the swelling. I taped up JD's ankle and wrapped it in an ace bandage before landing.

We left our gear and thanked the flight crew. I helped JD off the plane. He was walking a little better now, and with his arm over my shoulder, we ambled to the terminal.

We exited at the drop-off area, and I helped him off the curb. It only took an instant for me to notice Sophia had stopped. I looked over my shoulder at her standing on the curb.

She bit her bottom lip with a tormented look on her face.

"What's up?" I asked.

"I think this is where we go our separate ways."

JD balanced on his own as I took a step back to her.

"What's the matter? You tired of my company already?" I joked.

She chuckled. "No. I don't think I could tire of you that easily. But I'm not a fool. You've been good about reminding me that I'm a fugitive from the law. I know Isabella wants me dead, and she probably asked you to do it. I'm not stupid. But here I am. For some reason, you decided not to follow through."

I shrugged. "Everybody has a lapse in judgment at times."

She smirked and pulled the Russian passport from her pocket. "Thanks to Isabella, I have a new life awaiting. I've got a little money stashed in several offshore accounts. I can disappear and stay off the radar."

"You're going to retire?"

"I've been thinking about it for a while. I want to try *normal* for a bit. Settle down somewhere. Put down roots. Who knows?"

"Old assassins don't really put down roots."

"I'm not old." She paused and lifted a hopeful eyebrow. "You could always join me."

"This is where I belong."

"Look at who's put down roots."

"And you see how I have to look over my shoulder."

"I guess that's the price we pay, huh?"

I nodded.

She extended her hand and stood straight, trying to act professional. "It was fun, Deputy Wild."

I took her delicate hand. "It was certainly an adventure."

"Stay safe, Deputy. I hope you find that bomb before it goes off. Just don't get yourself blown up." She lifted on her tiptoes and kissed me on the cheek. It was soft and tender, almost like she cared.

"You'll find Holden Cauley at 1127 Grayling Lane." She spun around and marched back into the terminal to charter a flight. I watched her hips sway and wondered if that was the last time I would see her.

"Let's get it in gear!" JD yelled.

I helped him hobble across the lot and into the passenger seat of the Porsche. He gave me the keys, and I hopped behind the wheel. I cranked up the engine and dialed Sheriff Daniels. "You find anything?"

"Bomb squad has been through the *Seven Seas* multiple times. The dogs didn't find anything. The Coast Guard has gone boat to boat in the marina, searching every vessel on the water. They found no trace of an improvised nuclear device. Are you sure we're not on a wild goose chase?"

"I'm not sure of anything. I wouldn't put it past Fink to stir up drama over nothing."

"One last prank?" Sheriff Daniels suggested.

I backed out of the space and pulled out of the lot.

"The island was crawling with DHS and FBI," Daniels said. "When nothing turned up, most of them packed it in. You sure the ETC is the target?"

"It's gotta be. CEOs from every major energy company on the planet are all here for a weekend of schmoozing and boozing. You couldn't pick a better target. Think of the disruption to the sector."

"Think his goal was to spike energy prices?"

"I think his goal was disruption and destruction." I paused. "Where are the convention-goers now?"

"The hotel was temporarily evacuated. Since the dogs didn't find anything, they let everyone back in. The convention is proceeding as if this was a hoax."

"I've got a bad feeling about this," I said. "I don't think this was a hoax."

"I've got deputies at the hotel, keeping an eye on things. The convention has typically been running till 5 PM, then continues at the bar till the wee hours of the morning. Tonight there is a party around the pool."

"Were all the vehicles in the parking lot searched?"

"The dogs sniffed everything, and there were guys running around in hazmat suits with Geiger counters. This isn't my first rodeo."

"Maybe Fink's goon was full of shit?" JD said.

54

W e stopped by the marina at *Diver Down,* and I grabbed my badge and gun from the *Avventura.* I brought a backup for JD.

We headed to the *Seven Seas.* Deputy Frazier checked cars entering the parking lot. We stopped at the entrance and talked to him for a moment.

"Where's the K9 unit?" I asked.

"They split. I think they're at the airport."

"The airport isn't the target."

"Hey, I just work here," Frazier said.

"Have you seen anything odd?"

"Nothing out of the ordinary. I think this is a whole lot of nothing if you ask me."

We pulled into the lot, and I drove to the valet stand. Finding a parking space would have been damn near impossible. The place was packed. I flashed my badge and told the valet to keep it upfront.

JD climbed out of the car and hobbled around.

People milled about, and a few execs smoked cigarettes near the entrance. Deputy Bronson stood by the door.

"Maybe Fink's people were waiting for the final go-ahead from him," JD said.

I shook my head. "Once Fink puts a plan in motion, it stays in motion."

"We don't know that he's actually targeting the island," JD said. "That could have been a misdirection."

I was beginning to think he might be right. I was dreading the thought of hearing about an explosion at some other location that we hadn't considered.

I called Sheriff Daniels. "Let's get the dogs back here. I want every car that comes in this lot evaluated."

"As soon as they finish at the airport, I'll send them back."

"Is anyone guarding the hotel marina? Somebody could cruise right in and detonate a device. Why is nobody taking this seriously?"

Daniels was starting to get annoyed with my tone. "It was taken plenty seriously, and no threat was found. This whole thing is based on unconfirmed intel. The FBI and DHS have investigated and found no credible threat. What do you want me to do about it?"

"I have firsthand confirmation that something is going down."

"I believe you. But we can't secure the entire island. We don't have the resources."

"I'm telling you, this is the target. Whose bright idea was it to move the dogs away from this location?"

"It was mine," Daniels said with a tight jaw. "The airport is a viable target, and the Secretary of Energy will be landing at the FBO any minute. She's slated to give a speech at the close of the conference tomorrow, and her office requested a full sweep after hearing news of the threat. I'd say that's a high profile target and warrants consideration."

I couldn't argue.

"After her flight arrives, I'm sending the K-9 unit back to the Seven Seas. In the meantime, do what you do. Talk to your people and find out when and where this thing is going to hit."

Daniels ended the call, and I dialed Isabella. "What are you hearing?"

"Not a damn thing. With all these encrypted messaging apps, it's hard to get good intel. I'll let you know if I hear anything."

It wasn't long before a black limousine pulled into the parking lot with a police escort, red and blues flashing. The patrol unit and the limo pulled to the main entrance. They were followed by a black SUV with tinted windows.

Deputies hopped out and secured the area. The Secretary's security detail climbed out of the black SUV, scanned the area, did a quick check in the lobby, then returned to the limo and pulled open the passenger door.

The Secretary emerged wearing a navy blue blazer and skirt that hung past the knee. The security detail ushered her into the lobby.

Deputy Frazier waved a pool maintenance truck into the lot.

The 10-foot box truck rumbled around beside the entrance to the pool. The logo, surrounded by clear blue water, was painted on the side. The vehicle drew my eye right away.

The driver hopped out, wearing a jumpsuit and hat with the company logo. He moved around behind the vehicle and ambled down the pathway toward the pool.

I sprinted toward the vehicle, running past it, and held up at the pathway. I watched the pool maintenance guy pass through the gate and slip into the crowd of convention-goers. He weaved his way through to the far side, moving past lounge chairs, past the outside bar, and exiting toward the beach.

He wasn't here to maintain the pool.

The roll-up rear door to the box truck was padlocked shut. There was no doubt in my mind that there was a dirty bomb contained within.

A lawn maintenance guy was clipping branches with tree snips on the path to the pool. I raced toward him and flashed my badge. I grabbed the tree snips from the stunned man and raced back to the box truck.

It took a bit of force, but the padlock sheared free. I removed the linkage and carefully lifted the door, making sure it wasn't booby-trapped.

I didn't see a tripwire attached to the door, but my eyes widened with horror when I looked inside the box truck.

I didn't know how much time we had until detonation. I called Daniels and updated him on the situation.

The truck was filled with blue barrels with wiring that snaked around them from barrel to barrel. Sitting on top of it all was a small lead cylinder.

I climbed into the vehicle and began examining the construction of the bomb. I figured it was a pretty standard ammonium nitrate and fuel oil concoction. C-4 plastic explosive was used as the primary detonation charge, which would then detonate the more stable ANFO. It was all tied to a battery and a cell phone. A simple phone call would trip the phone's buzzer, which was powerful enough to trip a relay that would allow the battery to charge the blasting caps.

A phone call.

From anywhere in the world, at any time.

There was no timer.

No countdown.

It was both good and bad. I figured if someone was watching, they'd be inclined to detonate the device sooner rather than later. In the back of my mind, I hoped that Fink had planned on making the call himself.

That was wishful thinking.

I continued to study the device, looking for backup battery sources or additional cell phones. Sometimes bomb-makers will create decoys and redundant systems. Sometimes they won't.

I had disarmed a number of IEDs in my day, and it was always a nerve-racking experience. Time wasn't our friend in this scenario, and waiting for the EOD team wasn't an option.

Daniels had notified the other deputies, and they began evacuating the hotel, reassuring the guests this was just a precaution.

One discharge of static electricity could spell doom and trigger the device.

I touched the metal wall of the box truck, dissipating any charge that might have built up on my fingers. I held my breath and fumbled with the wiring, my heart pounding.

It was easy to disconnect the main battery. There wasn't any complicated wiring. When I did, the device didn't explode.

I breathed a sigh of relief and removed the blasting caps from the C4. Without the primary charges, the ANFO couldn't explode.

I climbed out of the vehicle, and the EOD team arrived shortly thereafter. Sergeant Hartman suited up in protective gear that made him look like an alien. He could barely climb into the back of the truck with the weight of the blast suit.

It didn't take Hartman long to determine that the device was rendered safe. He climbed out of the truck and pulled off the helmet—his face already dripping with sweat. "Good job, Wild. What about that lead container?"

"That's what worries me."

It wasn't long before Feds in hazmat suits with Geiger counters arrived.

The clickity-clack of the device increased when a man in a yellow bio- suit evaluated me. He didn't say a word, then climbed into the back of the truck, and the Geiger counter went a little more crazy when he scanned the lead cylinder.

After noodling around in the box truck for a minute, he hopped out and approached me. "We're definitely dealing with radioactive material."

"What about our exposure?" Hartman asked with a panic look on his face, sweat misting his brow.

56

"I don't want to grow a third arm or have my balls shrivel up," Hartman said.

The guy in the hazmat suit looked at him flatly. "You have balls?"

Hartman scowled at him.

"Relax. The container is shielded. It's emitting about a day's worth of background radiation. Nothing to worry about. Now, if you open the container, you'll be in a world of hurt."

We let the Feds clean up the mess. It was their problem to dismantle and dispose of the explosives. And they were equipped to handle the radioactive material. There would be a full investigation into its origin.

Slowly the guests began filtering back into the hotel now that the threat had been managed.

I drove JD to the hospital, where they did an X-ray and an MRI on his ankle. He sprained it, and the doctor prescribed anti-inflammatories, Tylenol for pain, and put him in a boot for a few weeks.

We headed to the station, filled out after-action reports, then I dropped JD off at his house. I pulled his Porsche up the circular drive to the entrance. He used his new crutches to hobble inside, and I helped him get situated.

"You need anything before I go?" I asked.

"I'm good. I think I'm gonna dial up a few honeys and have them nurse me back to health."

I chuckled. I had no doubt JD would be back in action in no time. "Just don't sprain anything else," I said before leaving.

I left his car in the driveway and caught a rideshare back to the marina.

The animals were with Teagan, and I had the evening to myself. I took a hot shower, poured myself a drink, and lounged around watching television, feeling mighty accomplished. There was one less terrorist in the world.

I still had enemies around the globe. There were plenty of angry cartel members and perps that I had put away. But I figured I'd get a pretty sound sleep tonight. There was no immediate threat.

I happened to catch an episode of celebrity homes. I was about to change the channel when I realized they would be featuring Nolan Orton's mansion in Stingray Bay. The episode had been filmed when he first moved to the island and transferred headquarters. At the time, there had been lots of talk about the island becoming the next Silicon Valley.

Nobody really wanted the influx. The locals liked the island just the way it was. We didn't want more traffic, more high-rises, and more crime—all the things that go along with a growing city.

The camera moved through the house, gliding effortlessly, showcasing the spacious design, the blending of the interior and exterior spaces, the fine furniture, the luxurious appointments. It showed the masses a lifestyle most would never have.

There were brief appearances by Nolan and Eva, discussing some of the personal touches they made to the house. With the recent news of her death, the previously aired episode became timely again.

The camera showed views of the bathrooms and the master bedroom. That's when I noticed something pertinent to the case.

At the foot of the bed was the brown steamer trunk. I was sure it was the same one Eva had been discovered in. The same one that Orton denied owning.

It was just the thing I needed to tie him to the case.

I called Sheriff Daniels right away. "We need a warrant to arrest Nolan Orton. I caught his ass in a lie."

The sheriff seemed intrigued.

I called JD. Crutches or no crutches, he wasn't about to miss this. I called for a rideshare to JD's, then drove the Porsche to the station. I made a sworn affidavit, and Daniels took it to the judge.

Surprisingly, Echols approved the warrant.

We put a tactical team together that included Mendoza, Robinson, Faulkner, and Erickson, and headed to Stingray Bay.

Several county vehicles pulled to the curb in the posh neighborhood. We all hopped out and advanced toward the home.

JD hobbled to the walkway.

I rang the bell at the gate, and Nolan answered a few moments later. "I've got nothing to say to you without the advice of counsel, Deputy. I thought I made that abundantly clear."

"We have a warrant for your arrest. We can do this the easy way or the hard way. It's up to you."

Nolan didn't respond right away.

57

"I didn't kill my wife," Nolan said.

He was silent for a long moment.

"Do I have to break down the gate?"

There was no response.

Just as Erickson and Faulkner were about to hammer it with a battering ram, the gate buzzed open, and we flooded into the courtyard.

Nolan opened the door and surrendered himself.

Erickson wrenched his arms behind his back and slapped the cuffs around his wrists. I read him his rights while the officers dragged him down the walkway and stuffed him into the back of a patrol car.

JD stood on the sidewalk, leaning on his crutches, watching with glee.

Nolan was taken to the station, processed, printed, and stuffed into an interrogation room. We let him stew for an hour, then decided to harass him. I pulled open the door, and JD hobbled in. I followed after him, and we took a seat across the table from Nolan.

Nolan looked less than thrilled about his current situation.

"Now is your chance to start talking," I said. "You lied to me about the steamer trunk. What else did you lie to me about?"

Nolan was stoic for a long moment. He sat there, contemplating his fate, trying to figure a way out of this. I figured he was too smart to talk to us. But sometimes arrogance takes over, and suspects think they can talk their way out of anything.

"I didn't kill my wife," Nolan said. "It was an accident."

"I'm listening."

"Things were tense between Eva and me, as you can imagine. We were fighting a lot. That day, we got into it pretty heavily. We were in the master bathroom, and she flew into a rage. She started punching me and pounding my chest. I pushed her away from me. I had no choice. She was physically attacking me."

He was trying to make himself sound like the victim, and I wasn't buying it.

"She fell back and hit her head on the corner of the counter," he continued. "It knocked her unconscious. My God, the blood. The blood was everywhere, oozing from her scalp." He paused, then stammered. "I thought she was dead. You have to believe me. She looked dead." His wide eyes pleaded for understanding.

"Did you check for vitals?"

He shook his head. "I called for Jason. He joined me in the bathroom. He knelt down beside Eva, felt for a pulse, and concluded that she was not alive."

I exchanged a wary glance with JD.

"So, the two of you panicked and conspired to dispose of the body," I said.

"Jason said he would take care of it. With everything that happened recently, and Eva wanting a divorce, I didn't think anybody would believe my story." His eyes begged for sympathy. "I thought she was dead. It was Jason's idea. He concocted the whole story. I went along with it. I figured what was the harm? Nothing I did was going to bring her back. We emptied the steamer trunk, carried it to the bathroom, then loaded her body inside. We sealed it up, and Jason thought it was best if I left with the two other bodyguards. That would give me plausible deniability. I could say I wasn't around. What happened after that, I don't know for sure. Jason said he loaded her into his truck, took her to his boat, then dumped her at sea."

"While she was still alive," I added.

"I didn't know that at the time. Had I known, I would have called 911, and maybe we could have saved her. I feel terrible about that."

"Well, you'll have a long time to think about it."

"But I didn't kill her."

"I guess it's up to a jury now, isn't it?"

"Can't you give me some type of a deal? All I did was help dispose of the body."

"Is that all?"

I didn't know how much, if any, of his story was true. And it really didn't matter. He admitted to several felonies, and he was going away for a long time.

We left the interrogation room, and I figured Nolan Orton would thoroughly enjoy his first night in jail. It would be a far cry from the accommodations he was used to.

We filled out after-action reports, then called it a night. I dropped JD off at home. He told me to keep the Porsche overnight. At this point, he wasn't worried about me wrecking it. *How much more damage could I do to it?* I drove back to the marina, ambled down the dock to the *Avventura,* and settled in for the evening.

The next day, we decided to investigate Sophia's claim.

1127 Grayling Lane was in an older neighborhood. The home that previously existed on the site had been demolished, and the lot had sat empty for almost a year until the new construction began last month. Nestled between lush foliage and tall palm trees was a newly poured foundation slab.

Slowly but surely, the old homes in the neighborhood were getting replaced with new builds.

I parked the Porsche at the curb, and we ambled up the walkway, JD still hobbling along on crutches.

"Are you thinking what I'm thinking?" JD asked.

I nodded.

I called Daniels, and he met us on site with cadaver dogs. The dogs sniffed the entire area and never indicated once.

"Let's grab the ground-penetrating radar," I said.

JD had an assortment of treasure hunting toys. The device sent electromagnetic waves through the ground and could detect anomalies in the soil up to 50 feet, depending on the composition. Sand, granite, and concrete didn't absorb the frequencies like clay and shale did. Sometimes you'd be lucky to see a foot below the surface in high absorption areas.

The device had a sophisticated algorithm to interpret the data and form a 3D image. It was a bulky, heavy piece of equipment that resembled a high-tech lawnmower with display screens.

"Do you really want to push the issue?" JD muttered. "I mean, what's the point?"

"I'd like to know if Sophia was telling the truth."

"What does it matter now?"

"If there's a body here, we need to find it."

In JD's current condition, he wouldn't be much help loading it in. I recruited Mendoza, and we headed to JD's house, grabbed the ground-penetrating radar from the garage, and loaded it into the back of the Wild Fury van.

I drove it back to Grayling, and we unloaded the device and rolled it to the foundation. Inch by inch, I covered every square foot, looking for anomalies under the surface. It was hard to determine what exactly was underneath the slab. When soil has been dug up, it packs in loosely afterward and has a different density compared with undisturbed soil. Since the whole area had been disrupted during construction, it was a little more difficult to determine what exactly was in the ground under the slab. But there was *something* down there about the right size and shape.

We all huddled around the display screen, trying to make heads or tails out of the image.

Daniels frowned. He pulled me aside and muttered, "And you have good intel that there's a body down there?"

I nodded.

"I don't want to dig up the slab only to find the remains of a dead dog or nothing at all."

"I think we're going to find the remains of Holden Cauley."

"And your *friend* confessed to the murder and gave you the location of the body?"

"Something like that."

"And you just let her walk away?"

"It was a complicated situation." Then I added, innocently, "And Cauley was a bad man."

Daniels glared at me for a moment. He shouted to the other deputies, "Okay. Let's dig this up."

Daniels coordinated a crew to start breaking up the concrete. Just as they were about to demo the pristine foundation, the property owner showed up.

58

"What the hell is going on here?" the landowner shouted with a distressed face.

"We're conducting an investigation," Daniels said.

"Not on my property, you're not."

"We have reason to believe there may be human remains on the premises."

The man's face tensed. "Do you have a warrant?"

Daniels didn't respond.

"If you don't have a warrant, I want you to get off my property, now!"

"And your name is?"

"I'm the landowner and the developer."

"Your name, sir?"

He huffed. "I don't have to tell you anything. You're on private property, and I would like you to leave."

"You're not the subject of the investigation," Daniels said, trying to calm the man.

"I don't care. I have a prospective buyer coming to look at the lot this afternoon. I don't want you anywhere around here. And I certainly don't want you demolishing my foundation. It cost a lot of money to put down." He leaned in and spoke in a hushed tone. "Do you know how hard it is to sell a property where someone's been killed?"

"We don't believe the victim was killed at this location."

"I don't care. I want you all out of here. Now!"

Daniels stared the man down for a moment, then sighed. "Alright, boys. Let's wrap this up."

The sheriff turned his attention back to the real estate developer and forced a smile. "I apologize for any inconvenience."

He didn't mean it.

The man glared at us as we left the property.

We headed back to the station, and Daniels attempted to get a warrant, but Judge Echols wouldn't sign off on it. He said that since the cadaver dogs didn't indicate, there was no compelling evidence to continue the search, despite my sworn affidavit and the *inconclusive* radar image.

I figured I would never know if Sophia was telling the truth. But Holden Cauley never did take another contract for murder.

Maybe he retired.

If he was underneath that slab, it wasn't a bad thing. He was a killer, no doubt about it. But I felt sorry for the people who bought the home.

After a few weeks, JD ditched the crutches and was getting along pretty well with the boot. His injury had put our treasure hunting on hold. He wasn't in any condition to fin around at the bottom of the ocean with a bum ankle. We took the opportunity to hang out, drink beer, and fish.

Wild Fury played their show, and Crash pulled himself together. He seemed to be staying away from the hard stuff and kept his drinking in moderation. The concert was a crowd-pleaser, despite JD's lack of mobility. Of course, Jack used his injury to solicit as much sympathy as he could from the opposite sex. He had no shortage of beauties willing to nurse him back to health.

It was a good few weeks. *Ultra Mega 2* was maintaining its reign at #1 atop the box office. Jack's daughter, Scarlett, had become a bonafide international celebrity overnight. She was in for a wild ride. I hoped she could handle it.

The summer was winding down, and things seemed almost normal.

Daniels called early one morning, and by the tone of his voice, I knew it wasn't good. "You are not going to believe this shit."

At this point, nothing surprised me anymore. I listened as he gave me the details. This was the start of no ordinary case.

Ready for more?

The adventure continues with Wild Island!

Join my newsletter and find out what happens next!

AUTHOR'S NOTE

Thanks for all the great reviews!

I've got more adventures for Tyson and JD. Stay tuned.

If you liked this book, let me know with a review on Amazon.

Thanks for reading!

—*Tripp*

TYSON WILD

Wild Thunder

Wild Season

Wild Rage

Wild Heart

Wild Spring

Wild Outlaw

Wild Revenge

Wild Secret

Wild Envy

Wild Surf

Wild Venom

Wild Island

Wild...

CONNECT WITH ME

I'm just a geek who loves to write. Follow me on Facebook.

www.trippellis.com

Made in the USA
Monee, IL
29 August 2021